The Tiger in the Tunnel

Ruskin Bond is known for his signature simplistic and witty writing style. He is the author of several bestselling short stories, novellas, collections, essays and children's books; and has contributed a number of poems and articles to various magazines and anthologies. At the age of twenty-three, he won the prestigious John Llewellyn Rhys Prize for his first novel, *The Room on the Roof*. He was also the recipient of the Padma Shri in 1999, Lifetime Achievement Award by the Delhi Government in 2012, and the Padma Bhushan in 2014.

Born in 1934, Ruskin Bond grew up in Jamnagar, Shimla, New Delhi and Dehradun. Apart from three years in the UK, he has spent all his life in India, and now lives in Landour, Mussoorie, with his adopted family.

The Tiger in the Tunnel

Edited and compiled by
RUSKIN BOND

Published by
Rupa Publications India Pvt. Ltd 2019
7/16, Ansari Road, Daryaganj
New Delhi 110002

Sales centres:
Bengaluru Chennai
Hyderabad Jaipur Kathmandu
Kolkata Mumbai Prayagraj

Copyright © Ruskin Bond 2019

This is a work of fiction. Names, characters, places and incidents are either the product of the author's imagination or are used fictitiously and any resemblance to any actual person, living or dead, events or locales is entirely coincidental.

All rights reserved.
No part of this publication may be reproduced, transmitted, or stored in a retrieval system, in any form or by any means, electronic, mechanical, photocopying, recording or otherwise, without the prior permission of the publisher.

P-ISBN: 978-93-5333-369-0
E-ISBN: 978-93-53333-70-6

Seventh impression 2025

10 9 8 7

The moral right of the author has been asserted.

Printed in India

This book is sold subject to the condition that it shall not, by way of trade or otherwise, be lent, resold, hired out, or otherwise circulated, without the publisher's prior consent, in any form of binding or cover other than that in which it is published.

CONTENTS

Introduction		vii
1.	The Langra Tigress *Hugh Allen*	1
2.	Tiger, Tiger, Burning Bright *Ruskin Bond*	24
3.	The Pale One *John Eyton*	53
4.	The Leopard *Ruskin Bond*	66
5.	Caulfield's Crime *Alice Perrin*	74
6.	Down Elephant Street *K.M. Eady*	85
7.	Panther's Moon *Ruskin Bond*	93
8.	Man-Eater *Frank Buck with Edward Anthony*	125
9.	The Chakrata Cat *Ruskin Bond*	147

10.	Eyes of the Cat *Ruskin Bond*	151
11.	Toomai of the Elephants *Rudyard Kipling*	154
12.	The Tiger in the Tunnel *Ruskin Bond*	177
13.	Rikki-Tikki-Tavi *Rudyard Kipling*	183
14.	'Sandy' Beresford's Tigerhunt *Charles A. Kincaid*	203
15.	The Vengeance of Kurnail Jarn *Jan Kinnsale*	211

INTRODUCTION

'The time I spent in the jungles held unalloyed happiness for me, and that happiness I would now gladly share. My happiness, I believe, resulted from the fact that all wildlife is happy in its natural surroundings. In nature there is no sorrow, and no repining. A bird from a flock, or an animal from a herd, is taken by hawk or carnivorous beast and those that are left rejoice that their time had not come today, and have no thought of tomorrow.'

—Jim Corbett

There was a time when shikar was acceptable as a sport or for commercial reasons or for protection. The walls of old houses lined with mounted heads and horns were a common sight. That helped in decimating the wildlife population, particularly of large predators like tigers and lions. As a boy, I have been part of hunting expeditions, when I chose to spend most of the time in the forest bungalow, my head in a book rather than in the jaws of a tiger.

If you don't have the time to visit a real jungle, the next best thing is to read about one. And to read about it when written about by someone who understands and loves wildlife is a joyful experience. In this collection, I have put together stories written by the greats and a few by yours truly. From Rudyard Kipling and Alice Perrin to Hugh Allen and Charles Kincaid, among many others—these writers will lure you to the jungle with its thick canopies, waterholes and grasslands; the call of the birds and the cries of the monkeys; and the spotting of presence panthers and mighty tigers.

Fact or fiction, these stories should make for some fascinating reading for my readers, of that I am sure. But what I want you to remember is that it is possible to exist in harmony with animals. Most wild animals do not harm humans unless provoked. Yet man tries to kill them, for his greed or honour. Our animals are the very soul of our culture and when the last of them goes, so will the soul of our country. I'd like to end this introduction with a D.H. Lawrence quote: 'There was room in the world for a mountain lion and me.' And now you may turn the page over and lose yourself in these magical jungles.

Ruskin Bond

THE LANGRA TIGRESS

Hugh Allen

Whenever I look back on the incident now, I wonder what might have happened if I had fired at the Langra Tigress the first time I saw her. Certainly she gave me the chance: The sort of chance that sportsmen often dream about yet so seldom get in reality. And I ought to have been ready and waiting to take it; for there had been plain warning that she was about. Even so, I was taken by surprise. Yet if I had been ready, I think it is very doubtful if I should have been able to write this story.

On the evening that this first encounter took place, I had gone out after a wild pig. For we are farmers, and our estate is situated in what were the old Central Provinces of India. That year we were planting a crop of groundnut over about a hundred acres of land which had just been cleared of thick jungle. It was something of an emergency measure. Coming Land Reforms threatened to take this area away from us unless it was put under cultivation. And since a considerable block of our forests had already been ceded to the government, we were trying to save the rest of the estate by complying quickly with the new regulations. But everything had been *very* hurried:

So much so, that for this crop there would be no fences round the fields.

That was the trouble. Wild boars and their sows love groundnuts. So, just before planting-time, I hoped to spread enough alarm and despondency among these pests to keep them away from the new fields until the seeds were in and had germinated. For if the swine are given the chance, they will run their iron-like snouts down the fresh drill-lines the night the seeds are put in; sucking up the nuts as they go along like mobile vacuum cleaners. Once the crop is above ground, it is fairly safe until half-ripe. Then the pigs again become an unmitigated nuisance.

It was a stifling, hot-weather evening when I prepared to go out. The rains were due to break at any moment, most probably early that night; for even as I was leaving the house, angry black clouds were building up rapidly above the distant, shimmering blue hills.

Just before I set off, the call of peafowl, coming from the direction in which I was going, had decided me to take a twelve bore shotgun—for the larder was low. And as the area for which I was bound was thick scrub jungle, buck-shot would be the most effective ammunition to sling against any pig I put up.

Through this ground there runs a small, twisting nullah, about 10-feet wide and 6 deep. I dropped down to the sandy bed. The banks are lined with many kinds of jungle tree: Some were already in full leaf, while others were performing that yearly miracle of producing delicate little green leaves and buds when it seemed impossible that there could be any moisture in that rock-like soil.

Peafows are very difficult to surprise: But a stalk along that soft, sandy bed could be made in absolute silence; and this place was a favourite haunt of these gallinaceous birds. Slowly I began to creep forward—and I had only been going about ten minutes when, cautiously rounding a sharp bend, I was suddenly stopped dead.

Just in front of me, apparently asleep under, a patch of shade, was a large leopard stretched out on the sand. But a closer look showed that something was wrong: its attitude was most unnatural; the head was twisted, and one forepaw was slightly bent and held drunkenly in the air. The animal was dead.

Moving swiftly up to it, my nose told me that it was very dead indeed. A swarm of blue flies burred up at my approach, wafting the sickly sweet smell of death more strongly to my nostrils. Some animal had eaten a small part of the hindquarters, and all round the sand was wildly churned up—but it was too soft to show any tracks. I began to look about me.

At once I spotted something else. A little farther down the nullah, and pulled in right under the bank, were the remains of what had once been a young chital stag. All that was left of it was the head, a few pieces of skill and splintered bone, and two almost whole ribs.

Both animals had been dead for about two days, and I began to wonder just what had happened. Then, looking round again for some definite clue, I saw ghat a small flame-of-the-forest tree had fallen across the bed of the nullah, and was blocking the view in that direction. I went up to it and looked across. Immediately something black caught my eye, lying almost at my feet, but on the other side of the tree: It was the dead body of a huge wild boar.

I climbed over and began to examine it. The mask was set in the most hideous snarl, and the one large tush I could see was not white, but stained brown with congealed blood. The remains were fresh, the meat hardly tainted; but some part of the hindquarters had been eaten, and the rest of the boar had been horribly ripped and torn. This was undoubtedly the work of a tiger, and by the look of things, he had not had it all his own way.

Then a very sinister fact penetrated to my mind. There was a complete absence of vultures or crows about any of the kills, and the jungle was ominously silent. Somewhere, close at hand, that tiger was lying up: It *must* be, or the nearby trees and the ground would have been thick with these revolting scavengers.

It was now just six o'clock, and a little darker than usual; for the black clouds had crept up overhead, and muffled thunder was vibrating in the hot, stifling air. This was a very likely time for the tiger to return for a feed, and the bed of that nullah was a very unhealthy spot. Rather hastily I climbed the bank and stood beside a small clump of saplings. The scrub jungle was very thick; for the previous year it had been cut over, and now, with the amazing rapidity with which the forests revive, the old stumps had sent up shoots to a height of several feet, and visibility was reduced to a few yards in any direction. Once up on the higher ground, I began to listen—complete silence. At the same time I was looking around for a suitable tree, covering the nullah, in which I might sit. For I felt sure that the tiger would return; most probably very soon.

But had it *already* seen or heard me?

There was not a rustle, or any other warning sound from the jungle; only the awakening evening insects broke the silence. And while I listened, I tried to put together the pieces of the story of that small nullah. That a tiger had killed the boar, I knew—but what of the leopard and the young chital stag? It was the most fascinating little mystery that I had ever come across.

Then, without a sound, the tiger suddenly appeared about five yards in front of me.

It was, rather, a tigress; and she came from behind a small cluster of teak like a conjurer's illusion. At first instance she did not see me, for she was moving obliquely *away*. But I must have made some slight movement of surprise, for suddenly she turned her head and looked straight at me. Yet it seemed that she did not notice me at all: Her eyes looked quite vacant, and in the calmest manner she continued on her way and passed out of sight behind some cover. As she went, I saw she was plastered with dried mud, along her left flank ran a long, bloody gash, and she was walking with a decided limp.

To this day I cannot understand why that tigress's sudden arrival was such a surprise to me. She so obviously had to be somewhere close. Yet, when she came, I was caught completely off my guard and made no effort to bring her down. An easier target could hardly have been imagined; but had I fired instinctively, it might well have been, for two reasons, the last trigger I ever squeezed.

The moment after that mud-stained body had disappeared from sight, I recovered my wits as there was still a good chance of collecting her. After the blistering heat of the day, and the pain of the wound, she would be making for water. Certainly she was headed in the right direction; for there was a pool, about fifty yards away, on the bed of another and larger nullah. If I could come upon her there, she would be a sitting shot from the high bank above.

I gave her a minute's start, then followed softly. About twenty yards to my front was a little clearing among the trees; on the farther side the ground rose steeply, and was covered with young saplings. Corning into the open space, I stopped and looked around: There was nothing in sight.

I was about to go on when a sudden, startling thought made me pause. I had been acting like a lunatic ever since I found that butcher's shop in the small nullah; for I had completely forgotten that I was carrying a shotgun, loaded, at that moment, with number six in the right barrel and buckshot in the choke. In mitigation, I can only plead that almost invariably I carry a .375 when out in the jungles, and the recent, unusual events were filling my mind to the exclusion of all else.

It was a mistake easily rectified. I had one lethal ball cartridge with me; so breaking the gun, I took out the number six and fished about in my pocket until I found the case I wanted.

Then, without any warning at all, everything happened at once. There was a shattering roar from the high ground a little to my right, and I heard the tigress crashing towards me through rough teak-leaves under the cover of the trees. The next second she came into view, and, with one mighty bound, landed in the clearing about thirty paces in front of me.

The shock was so complete that I was temporarily paralysed, and the ball cartridge dropped from my fingers as I was putting it in the chamber. This folly, I believe now, undoubtedly saved my life; for if the gun had been properly loaded, I am sure I should have used it in the next few confused minutes.

Because, for a second or two, I failed to appreciate the situation: Then, when I did, it came as another, stunning shock. The animal before me now was not the tigress—but a very large and most aggressive tiger! And he was obviously bent on mischief: There was little doubt about that; for as soon as he landed on his feet, he whipped about to face me—and then began weaving quickly from side to side across my front. At the same time he threw up his head and rent the air with a series of shaking, bellowing roars. More alarming still were the lightning-quick, feint attacks he began to make—all at once crouching low to the ground, hindquarters slightly raised, and ears laid back hard against his head, the lips mouthing a vicious snarl that rumbled out between gleaming fangs. Then, confidently, like a cat with a mouse in its power, he broke off his pantomime with a great sideways leap, to frisk off again—weaving and roaring.

At any second that tiger could come in: Each time he threatened, my eyes were focussed on the end of his tail. The moment that flickered—he would spring.

All this time I had been creeping slowly backwards, fascinated by that prancing striped yellow body. The shotgun still hung open over my left arm. Should I suddenly snap it shut and try for his head with the buckshot in the choke barrel? It might come off but it was a very long shot indeed.

Then I saw something that ruled this idea right out. From the corner of my eye I suddenly spotted the tigress. She was sitting up like a big domestic cat before a fire, just a few yards to my right, under a small kakra tree. And she was watching the scene before her with a pleased, gentle smile on her face.

When I saw her, I realized that the situation was well-nigh hopeless; everything became unpleasantly clear—these two were mating. That explained her extraordinary behaviour when she had seemed to ignore my presence, so near the kills, a little while earlier. For it is not uncommon, when the female is in season, to find her going about in a kind of dazed, ecstatic trance.

There was no hint of any ecstatic trance about the male! He undoubtedly meant business—if anything, he was getting more excited. For this encounter was just what he wanted: It was giving him an excellent opportunity to show-off before his sweetheart; and if that charnel house in the nullah was anything to go by, this tiger had put in quite a lot of practice.

I was still moving slowly backwards, but the tiger had decreased the distance between us. Suddenly I came up against a small tree, so I began to edge round the slender trunk; at last I had reached the limits of that little clearing. But this could not go on: Something must happen soon; indeed, it was surprising that the tiger had already waited so long.

Help came from the most unexpected quarter. A thin tongue of lightning flickered down in a brilliant, violet flash, and this was followed almost instantaneously by a mighty crash of thunder right overhead. It stopped the tiger dead in his tracks; then he looked about him, seemingly puzzled. The rain came hard on the thunder: first, a few large drops spattered against my hat and bare arms; then, only a moment later, the deluge roared and hissed down with the noise of an express train.

A solid sheet of water was cascading before my eyes, and soon it was splashing up from the ground in a thin mist. Hastily taking advantage of this heaven-sent diversion, I moved farther behind the shelter of my tree. I could still see the tiger; but now it seemed as if all the ardour had been soaked right out of him as the rain rattled and bounced off his streaming back. Watching him closely, I put another buckshot cartridge in the right barrel and slowly closed the gun; then I slipped forward the safety catch.

But he had given up. With a great shake of his rain-soaked body he wheeled abruptly and trotted away. Almost at once the tigress joined him, and together they went bounding off towards some broken land to find shelter.

With that first downpour, the monsoon set in without the usual break. There followed for me a very busy period: All the planting had to be done, and there was less time to think about tigers. In any case, it was hardly likely that those two would hang about, for during the rains these animals seldom stay long in one spot. But I did, at odd times, think of the carnage in that nullah: I had never come across anything like it before. I believed that both tigers had surprised the leopard soon after he killed the stag. And spots (for some leopards are very bold indeed) may have refused to give way over his own kill. Then the tiger may have gone for him: Not so much for possession of the carcass as to show-off to his mate. The tiger had attacked the boar too; and, I think, found him a worthy antagonist as soon as the fight began. So the tigress may have waded in to help him, and got, for her trouble, that long gash on her side. But that is all supposition: There are many other possible solutions. Sometimes I picture the scene of what *might* have happened if I had shot the tigress as soon as I saw her. It is not unlikely that the tiger would have appeared, to see what all the noise was about, when I was bending over the dead body of his lady love, quite unsuspicious of any further developments. Mien, no thunderstorm in this world would have kept him off...

But the tigers did not move on. Almost immediately there broke out an orgy of cattle-killing all around us. And it seemed a senseless slaughter: few of the animals taken were eaten, and the tigers never went back to a kill after the first feed.

Then, one day—about four miles away—a man was attacked and done to death. Certainly his demise was caused by a tiger, or tigers, but the body was found intact; no part of it had been eaten. Nevertheless, almost immediately after, the dread cry began to ring through the forests: *Adam Khor! A* man-eater stalks abroad!

The news spread with amazing rapidity. But I did not believe that this was the work of a man-eating tiger. It seemed, on the evidence, more likely to have been the result of a sudden, chance encounter such as had befallen me; but this time the victim had been unlucky. And I think I was right: There were no further human kills—at least for a considerable time. So, as the cattle slaughter stopped too, the scare gradually died down.

All this time at least one tiger was still about, and remaining very much on the same beat. For very often during the nights there came the sure signs that some carnivore was patrolling the jungles; and on two occasions I came across recent kills. Several times also I found the fresh tracks of a tiger.

These were very interesting; for they showed that it was dragging its left hindleg. So it was reasonable to suppose that this was the tigress that had been wounded by the hoar. It was on account of this limp that she eventually acquired the name 'Langra'.

She gave us no trouble: her behaviour was exemplary. In fact, I was quite glad of her presence; for as the months went by, the ripening groundnuts began to attract the attention of the wild pigs. A good watchful tigress, with a known taste for pork, was of decided value; much more so, in some ways, than the night-watchmen we were employing. For these men just sat on high wooden platforms in the fields and drove away the marauding sounders with an occasional shout—if they happened to be awake.

One night, however, the Langra Tigress disgraced herself. On the other side of the river she dragged a man down from his platform; killed him, carried him off, and then ate some of his body. Or so went the report that came in to us.

In actual fact, she did nothing of this: She only got the blame for it. When rumour and panic had been sifted from the truth, there was no real evidence against her. Admittedly, I was late on the scene: The dead man was not one of our own people but lived in a village some distance away; and he was not found for a whole day and night, for nobody made any serious effort to look for him. Then, when he was eventually discovered in some thick jungle, heavy rains had washed away any clues there might once have been. The body had been so thoroughly savaged that it was very obviously not the work of a tiger; for that animal is a clean killer. It looked much more like the mess that a large, solitary wild boar leaves after a mad, berserk attack. But in this opinion I was definitely alone. Once again the cry of 'man-eater' rang through the jungles; and this time it went on ringing.

All our night-watchmen struck work, leaving the groundnut crop wide open to the invading sounders of pig. Nor would any arguments of mine make them change their minds. No others for a considerable distance around, they earnestly assured me, were now watching on their land after dark. Moreover, they also pointed out, all of them were family men.

Some other arrangement to guard the fields had to be made at once: They could not be left unwatched for even a single hour after dark. At such short notice the lot must inevitably fall on me; for only my sister and myself live on the estate besides the servants. Each night I would have to go round the groundnuts on foot and keep the pests away as best as I could, until some other solution was found. It was not a pleasant prospect; and the first night gave me a nasty taste of what I was in for. Indeed, I liked it so little that I had another go at the watchmen the following morning: But again I failed to shift them, they stubbornly refused all the inducements I held before their eyes. So I resolved to beat for the tigress—and made matters far worse than they already were. For the monsoon is no time for this kind of sport; the jungle is too thick, and gives the animals every chance to slip out of the drive and get away in the dense cover quite unseen.

I was grasping at straws; there was no certainty that the tigress was lying up anywhere near us. But on the second day we got her moving. I heard the excited shout go up as she was discovered. Then came an alarming medley of frightened screams and yells as she broke back, swiping one man out of the way, and treeing the rest like a lot of gibbering monkeys.

Now, that going back on her part was very strange; for she was being driven gently in the direction which all her natural instincts must have told her was the safest one—yet she deliberately chose the hard way out. But after that, beating was stopped, and I had no alternative except to settle down to the nightly patrols around the fields in earnest.

'Do not be so foolish, sahib!' warned old Sama, the head watchman. 'All the others round us have liven up their crops to the care of God—no one is going abroad after dark. And your land is particularly dangerous'

Unfortunately the old man was only too right: All the fields in which the groundnuts had been planted were the ones we had recently hacked out of the jungles. And to make matters more difficult, they were not yet consolidated, but scattered haphazardly throughout the forests wherever the soil had been good. So it meant a walk of nearly two hours—mostly through jungle—to visit each field in turn. This, was distinctly uninviting; for, apart from tigers, the estate holds leopards and bears, and the chances of disturbing these about their lawful occasions are much greater at night than during the day.

The scare lasted for three months. All that time the tigress was seldom away for long. And during this period I had to keep going after those pigs during darkness, just as soon as the sun had set. Nearly every night I learnt something new; for moving through a pitch-black jungle alone is very different from a daytime walk over the same ground. In the dark, although at first it may not be realized, the sportsman is almost entirely protected from danger by his sense of hearing. The number of small, insignificant sounds that will stop a man dead after dark would be disregarded during the day or, more likely, not even noticed.

The pigs were extraordinarily troublesome. One lone boar in particular was bad-tempered and very aggressive. He resented interference with his meals so much that on one occasion he charged me from the rear, and in the ensuing fracas removed my shorts. But I got the pigs under control and pursued them relentlessly throughout the nights from field to field, never allowing them to settle down for long.

After some weeks of this night stalking I began to have much more confidence in myself. I was quickly learning to ignore dozens of little sounds by finding out just what they were. And my shooting after dark improved too. In the early stages, I had wasted a great deal of ammunition on the pigs; now I was hitting them more often. Nearly every shot had to be taken off-hand, quickly, and at an animal (probably moving) that was illuminated only by the light of a torch mounted on the weapon. In practice I found that the maximum effective range, under these conditions, was not more than forty yards for a dead certain kill. Beyond this distance the torch showed little except the staring *eyes* of the animal looking into the beam; usually the body was quite invisible.

Tigers were never long absent from my thoughts: Nearly every night the jungle told of some carnivore on the prowl.

Whenever one was near, the night would be charged with an electric tension; as if the whole forest waited with bated breath. Then, at intervals, would come the sure and certain warnings. The sharp, grating rasp of the sambur, the high-pitched 'Wow-ou!—Wow-ou!' of the terrified spotted-deer; and if the monkeys started to send up their coughing and sneezing alarm from the tree-tops, some large cat was certain to be passing beneath them. On one occasion—it was so near that it froze me to the spot for a full half-hour—there came the sudden, bloodcurdling scream of the lone jackal. And he, nearly always, precedes a prowling tiger.

After a time I realized that the nights of alarm were rather too many to be normal. For one thing, we have not as many tigers as all that and, secondly, the rains were still on. Even if a tiger should choose to stay for long in one place, he generally works round some regular beat which may take him ten days or so to complete. Yet the Langra Tigress—and I felt certain it was she—was remaining almost static on the estate. Was she now so lame that she could hardly get about? If this was so, what the devil was she eating? Certainly she was not addicted to human flesh; for, apart from that one very doubtful incident, there had been no further kills. Neither was she worrying cattle any more, so, somehow, she must be hunting her natural food—the jungle game.

The answer was simple, when I knew it, and I should have thought of it much sooner; for I had held all the clues from the start. But had I known the truth earlier I should have been much more worried than I already was; for I liked to believe that the tigress haunting the land was a sporting one, and would never dreamt of interfering with the absurd, two-legged creature who made such a noise moving about her jungles.

The night on which I finally learnt the truth about the Langra Tigress was a dreary one of high winds and stinging, driving rain. It was difficult to hear anything above the howling of the storm; and without my hearing I was feeling completely lost, and moving about *very* slowly. At three o'clock in the morning the wind suddenly dropped and the dark clouds overhead began to break up, leaving clear patches of sky through which the stars shone down. Wet through and miserable, I was making my way across one of the regular fields of the farm which was down to tili—a valuable oil-seed crop. This too needed watching: sambur stags and their hinds relish it, nibbling off the juicy green pods, and at this time of the morning I was quite likely to find some of these animals near the edges of the field.

I was to be disappointed; for just then, the tigress, too, was taking an interest in those samburs. Suddenly, from the direction of the river, came the sharp, clear alarm call of a hind. She seemed to be about four hundred yards from where I was standing. Soon it became apparent that something unusual was going on; because the sambur continued to call for much longer than was ever normal, and all the while she was moving very slowly nearer to where I stood. Never have I heard such a long alarm—it lasted for a full fifteen minutes. Then, suddenly, her cries redoubled, carrying with them a pitiful, almost pleading note. Shortly came the end of that hind's agony.

From a patch of teak forest, away across the field, rose a sudden crash as though some heavy body had been hurled down upon yielding, leafy cover. A strangled cry went up, immediately stifled in the throat, then complete silence. But not for long— soon there was a heavy scuffling and rustling among the crisp, dripping undergrowth, and then something moved off, making a great scraping noise as it passed through the big, rough teak leaves; a large animal was carrying away some heavy burden. I continued to listen as the sounds died away—there was no doubt in my mind that I had just heard the Langra Tigress killing her prey. Slowly I moved across to find the scene of the tragedy. It was not difficult to discover: The torch lighted upon a large patch of trampled ground, in the midst of which were two wrecked teak saplings.

Then I saw the tracks. That sambur hind had been defeated from her very first alarm call; for she had been up against not *one* tiger—but *three!*

Or so she must have thought. Because in the soft earth of a game-path the pug-marks of the Langra Tigress were very clear; and now it was obvious why she had remained for so long. She was accompanied by two small cubs, and they were just at an age to be taught how to kill. With the death of that hind, they had recently completed another night's lesson. And somewhere, probably among the hills up in the north corner of the estate, the tigress must have found a snug retreat.

With this new-found knowledge I was even more careful than before on the night rounds; for now there was real danger of a sudden attack. It would be enough just to place myself, however innocently, between the mother and her cubs to invite trouble. No longer was it possible to believe that I was being helped with the pigs by a tigress with sporting instincts. About the only instincts the Langra Tigress possessed now were maternal—perhaps the most dangerous of all. From that time I always carried a twelve-bore as being the handiest weapon, with a ball cartridge in the right barrel and buckshot in the left.

Six more weeks went by and still our paths had not crossed as far as I knew. Soon the groundnuts would be ripe, and then I would be free to resume a normal life. Nor would I be sorry:

These night vigils had been something of a strain; and now, although the rains were over, bitter cold weather had set in which did nothing to make the patrols more pleasant.

I met the Langra Tigress again just before harvest time.

It was a brisk, frosty night, and very dark with a fine Scotch mist rising off the river. The pigs, as usual, had been troublesome, and I had a mile to go before reaching home. My way led through what we called 'Whistling Wood', a small patch of mixed jungle, in the middle of which stood an enormous pipal tree. Many years previously, one of the great limbs of this forest giant had been struck by lightning, and it stood out, just a charred and withered member, pointing barrenly up to the sky. Time and termites had hollowed it out, and in some peculiar way it had become endowed with a remarkable characteristic.

When the wind from a certain direction had built up to a proper strength, a low melodious note suddenly boomed out, sounding not unlike the opening bars of *Ave Maria* played on an organ. During the hours of darkness it was an eerie and rather frightening sound, if you did not happen to know just what it was. Even so, none of our jungle folk would go near the place after nightfall. And not only for this reason; for there lay in that little patch of jungle the ashes of a great hunter, whose last wish was to rest among the forests and animals he had loved so well. Local superstition had it that a shadowy figure was generally to be seen stalking through the trees, with a rifle at the ready. Certainly the animals were there to keep him company: That little spot was a veritable Piccadilly Circus of game-tracks and, at night, about the most dangerous place along my route.

On this night, as I came into Whistling Wood, an intermittent, fresh morning breeze was springing up from the river, and all around me the young saplings were dancing and bobbing to the soft music of the pipal tree. Quickly I passed through without hearing or seeing anything. On the far side of the wood, and almost backing on to it, was a field of groundnuts. Coming out into the open, I saw the hurricane lanterns among the crop winking through the thinning mist. I stopped to listen. Suddenly—and I did not see the direction from which they came—two jackals darted into the feeble circle of light thrown by the lantern nearest to me, about twenty-five yards off. Now jackals are another pest which attacks groundnuts, tearing up the nuts with their paws and eating them, and this field was, for some reason, more open to their visitations than any of the others.

For a moment I watched them idly. They were gambolling about round the edge of the feeble circle of light, and there was something very graceful about the way they played. Round and round they went—twisting and turning, rolling and wrestling; pausing, then dodging and chasing all over again. So full of life did they seem that I decided to forgive them. As I began to move off, I lit a cigarette, and as the match flickered, I thought idly that those animals played more like cats...

...*Cats!*

And then I *really* looked at them. Cats they were: little yellow ones with black stripes...Tiger cubs!

As soon as I was sure, I stood absolutely still. Where was their mother? Was she, in fact, *already* watching me? For up to that moment I had not been moving with a great deal of caution; and there was also that unfortunate cigarette. On the other hand she might not yet know of my presence—so I began to strain my ears to catch the slightest sound that might betray her. But that fresh breeze, playing with the leaves and trees, and boosting up the strains of *Ave Maria* from the wood behind me, was kicking up so much row that it must inevitably be masking any tiny sound that the tigress might make. Angry and frightened, I began to curse it heartily. But the next moment it told me where the Langra Tigress was.

The wind was blowing on to the right side of my face as I stood watching the cubs and listening. All at once—and it was but a fleeting impression—there whisked past my nostrils a distinct smell of tiger. There was no doubt about it—the scent of these animals cannot be confused with anything else on earth. Then, as if to confirm my nose, the tigress called sharply to her cubs from out of the darkness. That meant she had located me, or was, at least, very suspicious of some danger.

I raised the gun and switched on the torch. A light, I hoped, would confuse her. And being, most likely, right outside her experience, might persuade her to slink *away* with her precious brood without further incident.

Almost immediately I picked up her eyes in the beam of the torch. She was about thirty yards away. But the eyes were all I could see of her, because the torch batteries were becoming exhausted; they had just had a very hard night, and had not been new when I set out. The beam was just a dull *yellow* stab in the darkness with the eyes staring back from the end of it.

The tigress seemed to be moving very slowly: not directly towards me, but slightly and obliquely away. Without seeing her clearly, it was difficult to judge her intentions. Above all things I wanted to avoid risking a shot unless I had no other alternative. For it looked as if she was trying to make off. But I could not see her properly—if only the torch was a little brighter.

Automatically, with my left hand, I began to squeeze round the small switch which was strapped to the fore part of the gun:

From past experience I knew that this treatment sometimes resulted in a brighter light, as occasionally the contacts became dirty. Still keeping the eyes in the centre of the beam, I began to squeeze harder.

I have never been able to account satisfactorily for what happened next: Tensed up nerves certainly had something to do with it; that, and some unconscious sympathy shown by my right hand for what my left was doing—for, without in any way meaning to, I squeezed the right trigger.

Both recoil and report took me completely by surprise. And then, to my horror, as the noise of the explosion died away, I heard that low-velocity ball strike with a sickening *smack!* As it did so, the *eyes* vanished.

Appalled at what I had done, I stood and kept the light on the spot where the tigress had been. There was neither sound nor movement. After some time I began to think I had dropped her dead in her tracks. And this would not have been too much of a fluke; for the range was just over thirty yards, and the torch was so fixed that the shot would have passed down the middle of the beam. I waited a good ten minutes and then began to move slowly forward. But when I came near to where she ought to have been lying, there was nothing there. Nor, when I cast the light farther afield, was there any sign of her. Then I began to think I had missed, and that the shot had hit something else.

Now, by all the usual rules of tiger-shooting, it was asking for trouble to follow her up at once. But those rules were for straight-forward, daytime hunting; the present circumstances were exceptional. It was still very dark, and the safest thing to do was to find the tigress before she recovered from the first shock of that bullet—if indeed she had been hit—and launched an attack. For there was no clue to where she was, and it was useless for me to think of running away until daylight—any direction might bring me straight on top of her. So I had little alternative but to continue the search.

Soon, I came upon the first blood, glistening in the soft glow of the torch, smeared on a few kakra leaves which had been rolled on. I set off slowly along the blood trail, which soon became very distinct. But every minute the torch was getting weaker; at times it started to flicker.

Almost without warning, I nearly stumbled right into her. Fortunately she gave herself away: There came a quick choking growl from a little way ahead, and when I whipped up the light I saw the Langra Tigress clearly for the first time that night. She was crouched, a little to my right and about seven yards away, her ears lying flat and her lips drawn back in a savage snarl. But before I had properly seen her and blinded her with the light, I knew she had seen me too. So I raised the gun quickly... and she sprang straight for the torch as I pulled both triggers.

Instinctively, even as I fired, I had known that this was coming: So I believe I had started to throw myself madly sideways and down as she was leaving the ground. But something, and I think it was one of her hindpaws, caught me and sent me sprawling backwards. I heard her land with a soft thud close behind me. I still cannot remember all I did, or even what went on during the next few confused seconds; but somehow I got the torch on her again, and she answered this with a choking, gasping roar which seemed to burst right in my face. Now she was on the ground with only her head and shoulders raised: Obviously very badly wounded, but she was making a desperate and frantic effort to stand up—her great forepaws were clawing madly at the earth. Her hindlegs appeared to be useless; for the back part of her body was lying flat on the ground, and for all her furious attempts she was just dragging it slowly forward.

Keeping the light on her, I got quickly to my feet. All her violent, futile exertions told plainly of a broken back: A well-placed shot now would finish her. But the gun had only spent cases in the chambers. Never have I felt possessed of so many thumbs as I groped feverishly for cartridges. Right pocket, ball—left, buckshot…or was it the other way about…? For my jacket suddenly seemed to have gone crazy—then I found it was hanging in tattered shreds about me. Somehow the ammunition was found and rammed into the breeches. By this time, in spite of the intensely cold night air, sweat was streaming down my face, because all the time I had been frantically fumbling about, the tigress, like some fantastic horror out of a nightmare, had been striving violently to get at me. Then, as I roughly snapped the gun shut and jabbed the safety catch forward, she suddenly collapsed: Her head dropped to the ground, and she began to gasp in great lungfuls of air.

She was obviously finished: But it seldom pays to be too sure of any tiger that is still breathing. So, somewhat unsteadily, I crept round to her flank and put in another shot at the base of her skull. A little shiver ran through the massive body, then the mouth opened slowly, and—after a brief moment—as slowly closed for the last time. With a slight final tremor, the great head sank more firmly onto the ground.

Up to that moment I had acted like a man going through a fantastic dream, whose subconscious mind is telling him all the time that none of it is reality. Now it was over, my knees suddenly felt so weak I had to sit down on the ground. And to steady my nerves I lit a cigarette. While I was smoking it

I surveyed the damage to my zip jacket—the front had been torn right down. The thick scarf which I wore underneath had taken most of the punishment; apart from a—few scratches, I was unhurt.

I did not really deserve to get away so lightly: That first shot should never have been fired; there was no proper excuse for it at all I am quite certain now that if I had not fired, the tigress would have left me alone; for she had already called to her cubs and, as far as I could see, was making off, taking her precious brood away from that strange light beyond which she could see nothing. And who knows how many times she had seen me about before? Perhaps, after all these months, I had become quite a familiar figure to her, unknown to myself. If this were true, then she might very well have possessed all those sporting qualities with which I had once credited her.

As, I finished my cigarette, dawn was just painting the eastern sky with delicate hues of pink and lemon light. And, as the new day began, I reflected that the night patrols were over at last. Looking back on it...all, I could not truthfully say that I had enjoyed it, although I learnt a great deal. But when I thought of the tigress, and the boar that removed my pants, I realized that as a night hunter I still had a long way to go. For the encounters had been brought about by my own carelessness; and each time. I had been more lucky than I deserved. So, all things considered, I cannot recommend night-shooting on foot unless you have to do it...even if you avoid making the fat-headed mistakes that I made.

TIGER, TIGER, BURNING BRIGHT

Ruskin Bond

On the left bank of the Ganga, where it emerges from the Himalayan foothills, there is a long stretch of heavy forest. These are villages on the fringe of the forest, inhabited by bamboo cutters and farmers, but there are few signs of commerce or pilgrimage. Hunters, however, have found the area an ideal hunting ground during the last seventy years, and as a result the animals are not as numerous as they used to be. The trees, too, have been disappearing slowly; and, as the forest recedes, the animals lose their food and shelter and move on further into the foothills. Slowly, they are being denied the right to live.

Only the elephants can cross the river. And two years ago, when a large area of forest was cleared to make way for a refugee resettlement camp, a herd of elephants—finding their favourite food, the green shoots of the bamboo, in short supply—waded across the river. They crashed through the suburbs of Haridwar, knocked down a factory wall, pulled down several tin roofs, held up a train, and left a trail of devastation in their wake until they found a new home in a new forest which was still untouched.

Here, they settled down to a new life—but an unsettled, wary life. They did not know when men would appear again, with tractors, bulldozers and dynamite.

There was a time when the forest on the banks of the Ganga River had provided food and shelter for some thirty or forty tigers; but men in search of trophies had shot them all, and now there remained only one old tiger in the jungle. Many hunters had tried to get him, but he was a wise and crafty old tiger, who knew the ways of men, and he had so far survived all attempts on his life.

Although the tiger had passed the prime of his life, he had lost none of his majesty. His muscles rippled beneath the golden yellow of his coat, and he walked through the long grass with the confidence of one who knew that he was still a king, even though his subjects were fewer. His great head pushed through the foliage, and it was only his tail, swinging high, that showed occasionally above the sea of grass.

In late spring he would head for the large jheel, the only water in the forest (if you don't count the river, which was several miles away), which was almost a lake during the rainy season, but just a muddy marsh at this time of the year.

Here, at different times of the day and night, all the animals came to drink—the long-horned sambhar, the delicate chital, the swamp deer, the hyenas and jackals, the wild boar, the panthers—and the lone tiger. Since the elephants had gone, the water was usually clear except when buffaloes from the nearest village came to wallow in it, and then it was very muddy. These buffaloes, though they were not wild, were not afraid of the panther or even of the tiger. They knew the panther was afraid of their massive horns and that the tiger preferred the flesh of the deer.

One day, there were several sambhars at the water's edge; but they did not stay long. The scent of the tiger came with the breeze, and there was no mistaking its strong feline odour. The deer held their heads high for a few moments, their nostrils twitching, and then scattered into the forest, disappearing behind a screen of leaf and bamboo.

When the tiger arrived, there was no other animal near the water. But the birds were still there. The egrets continued to wade in the shallows, and a kingfisher darted low over the water, dived suddenly, a flash of blue and gold, and made off with a slim silver fish, which glistened in the sun like a polished gem. A long brown snake glided in and out among the waterlilies and disappeared beneath a fallen tree which lay rotting in the shallows.

The tiger waited in the shelter of a rock, his ears pricked up for the least unfamiliar sound; he knew that it was at that place that men sometimes sat up for him with guns, for they coveted his beauty—his stripes, and the gold of his body, his fine teeth, his whiskers, and his noble head. They would have liked to hang his skin on a wall, with his head stuffed and mounted, and pieces of glass replacing his fierce eyes. Then they would have boasted of their triumph over the king of the jungle.

The tiger had encountered hunters before, so he did not usually show himself in the open during the day. But of late he had heard no guns, and if there were hunters around, you would have heard their guns (for a man with a gun cannot resist letting it off, even if it is only at a rabbit—or at another man). And, besides, the tiger was thirsty.

He was also feeling quite hot. It was March, and the shimmering dust haze of summer had come early. Tigers— unlike other cats—are fond of water, and on a hot day will wallow in it for hours.

He walked into the water, in amongst the water lilies, and drank slowly. He was seldom in a hurry when he ate or drank. Other animals might bolt down their food, but they are only other animals. A tiger is a tiger; he has his dignity to preserve even though he isn't aware of it!

He raised his head and listened, one paw suspended in the air. A strange sound had come to him on the breeze, and he was wary of strange sounds. So he moved swiftly into the shelter of the tall grass that bordered the jheel, and climbed a hillock until he reached his favourite rock. This rock was big enough both to hide him and to give him shade. Anyone looking up from the jheel would have thought it strange that the rock had a round bump on the top. The bump was the tiger's head. He kept it very still.

The sound he heard was only the sound of a flute, rendered thin and reedy in the forest. It belonged to Ramu, a slim brown boy who rode a buffalo. Ramu played vigorously on the flute. Shyam, a slightly smaller boy, riding another buffalo, brought up the rear of the herd.

There were about eight buffaloes in the herd, and they belonged to the families of the two friends Ramu and Shyam. Their people were Gujars, a nomadic community who earned a livelihood by keeping buffaloes and selling milk and butter. The boys were about twelve years old, but they could not have told you exactly because in their village nobody thought birthdays were important. They were almost the same age as the tiger, but he was old and experienced while they were still cubs.

The tiger had often seen them at the tank, and he was not worried by their presence. He knew the village people would do him no harm as long as he left their buffaloes alone. Once when he was younger and full of bravado, he had killed a buffalo—not because he was hungry, but because he was young and wanted to try out his strength—and after that the villagers had hunted him for days, with spears, bows and an old muzzle loader. Now he left the buffaloes alone, even though the deer in the forest were not as numerous as before.

The boys knew that a tiger lived in the jungle, for they had often heard him roar; but they did not suspect that he was so near just then.

The tiger gazed down from his rock, and the sight of eight fat black buffaloes made him give a low, throaty moan. But the boys were there. Besides, a buffalo was not easy to kill.

He decided to move on and find a cool shady place in the heart of the jungle where he could rest during the warm afternoon and be free of the flies and mosquitoes that swarmed around the jheel. At night he would hunt.

With a lazy, half-humorous roar—'A-oonh!'—he got up off his haunches and sauntered off into the jungle.

Even the gentlest of the tiger's roars can be heard half a mile away, and the boys, who were barely fifty yards away, looked up immediately.

'There he goes!' said Ramu, taking the flute from his lips and pointing it towards the hillocks. He was not afraid, for he knew that this tiger was not interested in humans. 'Did you see him?'

'I saw his tail, just before he disappeared. He's a big tiger!'

'Do not call him tiger. Call him uncle, or maharaja.'

'Oh, why?'

'Don't you know that it's unlucky to call a tiger a tiger? My father always told me so. But if you meet a tiger, and call him uncle, he will leave you alone.'

'I'll try and remember that,' said Shyam.

The buffaloes were now well inside the water, and some of them were lying down in the mud. Buffaloes love soft, wet mud and will wallow in it for hours. The slushier the mud the better. Ramu, to avoid being dragged down into the mud with his buffalo, slipped off its back and plunged into the water. He waded to a small islet covered with reeds and water lilies. Shyam was close behind him.

They lay down on their hard flat stomachs, on a patch of grass, and allowed the warm sun to beat down on their bare brown bodies.

Ramu was the more knowledgeable boy because he had been to Haridwar and Dehradun several times with his father. Shyam had never been out of the village.

Shyam said, 'The pool is not so deep this year.'

'We have had no rain since January,' said Ramu. 'If we do not get rain soon the jheel may dry up altogether.'

'And then what will we do?'

'We? I don't know. There is a well in the village. But even that may dry up. My father told me that it did once, just about the time I was born, and everyone had to walk ten miles to the river for water.'

'And what about the animals?'

'Some will stay here and die. Others will go to the river. But there are too many people near the river now—and temples, houses and factories—so the animals stay away. And the trees have been cut, so that between the jungle and the river there is no place to hide. Animals are afraid of the open—they are afraid of men with guns.'

'Even at night?'

'At night men come in jeeps, with searchlights. They kill

the deer for meat, and sell the skins of tigers and panthers.'

'I didn't know a tiger's skin was worth anything.'

'It's worth more than our skins,' said Ramu knowingly. 'It will fetch six hundred rupees. Who would pay that much for one of us?'

'Our fathers would.'

'True—if they had the money.'

'If my father sold his fields, he would get more than six hundred rupees.'

'True—but if he sold his fields, none of you would have anything to eat. A man needs land as much as a tiger needs a jungle.'

'Yes,' said Shyam. 'And that reminds me—my mother asked me to take some roots home.'

'I will help you.'

They walked deeper into the jheel until the water was up to their waists, and began pulling up water lilies by the roots. The flower is beautiful but the villagers value the root more. When it is cooked, it makes a delicious and nourishing dish. The plant multiplies rapidly and is aways in good supply. In the year when famine hit the village, it was only the root of the water lily that saved many from starvation.

When Shyam and Ramu had finished gathering roots, they emerged from the water and passed the time wrestling with each other, slipping about in the soft mud which soon covered them from head to toe.

To get rid of the mud, they dived into the water again and swam across to their buffaloes. Then, jumping on to their backs and digging their heels into the thick hides, the boys raced them across the jheel, shouting and hollering so much that all the birds flew away in fright, and the monkeys set up a shrill chattering of their own in the dhak trees.

In March, the flame of the forest, or dhak trees, are ablaze with bright scarlet and orange flowers.

It was evening, and the twilight was fading fast, when the buffalo herd finally wandered its way homeward, to be greeted outside the village by the barking of dogs, the gurgle of hookah pipes, and the homely smell of cow-dung smoke.

The tiger made a kill that night—a chital. He made his approach against the wind so that the unsuspecting spotted deer did not see him until it was too late. A blow on the deer's haunches from the tiger's paw brought it down, and then the great beast fastened his fangs on the deer's throat. It was all over in a few minutes. The tiger was too quick and strong, and the deer did not struggle much.

It was a violent end for so gentle a creature. But you must not imagine that in the jungle the deer live in permanent fear of death. It is only man, with his imagination and his fear of the hereafter, who is afraid of dying. In the jungle it is different. Sudden death appears at intervals. Wild creatures do not have to think about it, and so the sudden killing of one of their number by some predator of the forest is only a fleeting incident soon forgotten by the survivors.

The tiger feasted well, growling with pleasure as he ate his way up the body, leaving the entrails. When he had had his night's fill he left the carcass for the vultures and jackals. The cunning old tiger never returned to the same carcass, even if there was still plenty left to eat. In the past, when he had gone back to a kill he had often found a man sitting in a tree waiting up for him with a rifle.

His belly filled, the tiger sauntered over to the edge of the forest and looked out across the sandy wasteland and the deep, singing river, at the twinkling lights of Rishikesh on the opposite bank, and raised his head and roared his defiance at mankind.

He was a lonesome bachelor. It was five or six years since he had a mate. She had been shot by the trophy hunters, and her two cubs had been trapped by men who do trade in wild animals. One went to a circus, where he had to learn tricks to amuse men and respond to the crack of a whip; the other, more fortunate, went first to a zoo in Delhi and was later transferred to a zoo in America.

Sometimes, when the old tiger was very lonely, he gave a great roar, which could be heard throughout the forest. The villagers thought he was roaring in anger, but the jungle knew that he was really roaring out of loneliness. When the sound of his roar had died away, he paused, standing still, waiting for an answering roar; but it never came. It was taken up instead by the shrill scream of a barbet high up in a sal tree.

It was dawn now, dew-fresh and cool, and jungle dwellers were on the move...

The black beady little eyes of a jungle rat were fixed on a brown hen who was pecking around in the undergrowth near her nest. He had a large family to feed, this rat, and he knew that in the hen's nest was a clutch of delicious fawn-coloured eggs. He waited patiently for nearly an hour before he had the satisfaction of seeing the hen leave her nest and go off in search of food.

As soon as she had gone, the rat lost no time in making his raid. Slipping quietly out of his hole, he slithered along among the leaves; but, clever as he was, he did not realize that his own movements were being watched.

A pair of grey mongooses scouted about in the dry grass. They, too, were hungry, and eggs usually figured large on their menu. Now, lying still on an outcrop of rock, they watched the rat sneaking along, occasionally sniffing at the air and finally vanishing behind a boulder. When he reappeared, he was struggling to roll an egg uphill towards his hole.

The rat was in difficulty, pushing the egg sometimes with his paws, sometimes with his nose. The ground was rough, and the egg wouldn't move straight. Deciding that the must have help, he scuttled off to call his spouse. Even now the mongooses did not descend on the tantalizing egg. They waited until the rat returned with his wife, and then watched as the male rat took the egg firmly between his forepaws and rolled over on to his back. The female rat then grabbed her mate's tail and began to drag him along.

Totally absorbed in the struggle with the egg, the rat did not hear the approach of the mongooses. When these two large furry visitors suddenly bobbed up from behind a stone, the rats squealed with fright, abandoned the egg, and fled for their lives.

The mongooses wasted no time in breaking open the egg and making a meal of it. But just as, a few minutes ago, the rat had not noticed their approach, so now they did not notice the village boy, carrying a small bright axe and a net bag in his hands, creeping along.

Ramu, too, was searching for eggs, and when he saw the mongooses busy with one, he stood still to watch them, his eyes roving in search of the nest. He was hoping the mongooses would lead him to the nest; but, when they had finished their meal and made off into the undergrowth, Ramu had to do his own searching. He failed to find the nest, and moved further into the forest. The rat's hopes were just reviving when, to his disgust, the mother hen returned.

Ramu now made his way to a mahua tree.

The flowers of the mahua can be eaten by animals as well as by men. Bears are particularly fond of them and will eat large quantities of flowers which gradually start fermenting in their stomachs with the result that the animals get quite drunk. Ramu had often seen a couple of bears stumbling home to their cave, bumping into each other or into the trunks of trees. They are short-sighted to begin with, and when drunk can hardly see at all. But their sense of smell and hearing are so good that in the end they find their way home.

Ramu decided he would gather some mahua flowers, and climbed up the tree, which is leafless when it blossoms. He began breaking the white flowers and throwing them to the ground. He had been on the tree for about five minutes when he heard the whining grumble of a bear, and presently a young sloth bear ambled into the clearing beneath the tree.

He was a small bear, little more than a cub, and Ramu was not frightened; but, because he thought the mother might be in the vicinity, he decided to take no chances, and sat very still, waiting to see what the bear would do. He hoped it wouldn't choose the mahua tree for a meal.

At first, the young bear put his nose to the ground and sniffed his way along until he came to a large anthill. Here he began huffing and puffing, blowing rapidly in and out of his nostrils, causing the dust from the anthill to fly in all directions. But he was a disappointed bear, because the anthill had been deserted long ago. And so, grumbling, he made his way across to a tall wild plum tree, and shinning rapidly up the smooth trunk, was soon perched on its topmost branches. It was only then that he saw Ramu.

The bear at once scrambled several feet higher up the tree, and laid himself out flat on a branch. It wasn't a very thick branch and left a large expanse of bear showing on either side. The bear tucked his head away behind another branch, and so long as he could not see Ramu, seemed quite satisfied that he was well-hidden, though he couldn't help grumbling with anxiety, for a bear, like most animals, is afraid of man.

Bears, however, are also very curious—and curiosity has often led them into trouble. Slowly, inch by inch, the young bear's black snout appeared over the edge of the branch; but immediately the eyes came into view and met Ramu's, he drew back with a jerk and the head was once more hidden. The bear did this two or three times, and Ramu, highly amused, waited until it wasn't looking, then moved some way down the tree. When the bear looked up again and saw that the boy was missing, he was so pleased with himself that he stretched right across to the next branch, to get a plum. Ramu chose this moment to burst into loud laughter. The startled bear tumbled out of the tree, dropped through the branches for a distance of some fifteen feet, and landed with a thud in a heap of dry leaves.

And then several things happened at almost the same time.

The mother bear came charging into the clearing. Spotting Ramu in the tree, she reared up on her hind legs, grunting fiercely. It was Ramu's turn to be startled. There are few animals more dangerous than a rampaging mother bear, and the boy knew that one blow from her clawed forepaws could rip his skull open.

But before the bear could approach the tree, there was a tremendous roar, and the old tiger bounded into the clearing. He had been asleep in the bushes not far away—he liked a good sleep after a heavy meal—and the noise in the clearing had woken him.

He was in a bad mood, and his loud 'A-oonh!' made his

displeasure quite clear. The bears turned and ran from the clearing, the youngster squealing with fright.

The tiger then came into the centre of the clearing, looked up at the trembling boy, and roared again.

Ramu nearly fell out of the tree...

'Good day to you, Uncle,' he stammered, showing his teeth in a nervous grin.

Perhaps this was too much for the tiger. With a low growl, he turned his back on the mahua tree and padded off into the jungle, his tail twitching in disgust.

That night, when Ramu told his parents and his grandfather about the tiger and how it had saved him from a female bear, it started a round of tiger stories—about how some of them could be gentlemen, others rogues. Sooner or later the conversation came round to man-eaters, and Grandfather told two stories which he swore were true, although his listeners only half believed him.

'The first story concerned the belief that a man-eating tiger is guided towards his next victim by the spirit of a human being previously killed and eaten by the tiger. Grandfather said that he actually knew three hunters who sat up in a machan over a human kill and when the tiger came, the corpse sat up and pointed with his right hand at the men in the tree. The tiger then went away. But the hunters knew he would return, and one man was brave enough to get down from the tree and tie the right arm of the corpse to its side. Later, when the tiger returned, the corpse sat up and this time pointed out the men with his left hand. The enraged tiger sprang into the tree and killed his enemies in the machan.

'And then there was a bania,' said Grandfather, beginning another story, 'who lived in a village in the jungle. He wanted to visit a neighbouring village to collect some money that was owed to him, but as the road lay through heavy forest in which lived a terrible man-eating tiger, he did not know what to do. Finally, he went to a sadhu who gave him two powders. By eating the first powder he could turn into a huge tiger, capable of dealing with any other tiger in the jungle, and by eating the second he would become a bania again.

'Armed with his two powders, and accompanied by his pretty, young wife, the bania set out on his journey. They had not gone far into the forest when they came upon the man-eater sitting in the middle of the road. Before swallowing the first powder, the bania told his wife to stay where she was, so that when he returned after killing the tiger, she could at once give him the second powder and enable him to resume his old shape.

'Well, the bania's plan worked, but only up to a point. He swallowed the first powder and immediately became a magnificent tiger. With a great roar, he bounded towards the man-eater, and after a brief, furious fight, killed his opponent. Then, with his jaws still dripping blood, he returned to his wife.

'The poor girl was terrified and spilt the second powder on the ground. The bania was so angry that he pounced on his wife and killed and ate her. And afterwards this terrible tiger was so enraged at not being able to become a human again that he killed and ate hundreds of people all over the country.

'The only people he spared,' added Grandfather, with a twinkle in his eyes, 'were those who owed him money. A bania never gives up a loan as lost, and the tiger still hoped that one day he might become a human again and be able to collect his dues.'

Next morning, when Ramu came back from the well which was used to irrigate his father's fields, he found a crowd of curious children surrounding a jeep and three strangers with guns. Each of the strangers had a gun, and they were accompanied by two bearers and a vast amount of provisions.

They had heard that there was a tiger in the area, and they wanted to shoot it.

One of the hunters, who looked even more strange than the others, had come all the way from America to shoot a tiger, and he vowed that he would not leave the country without a tiger's skin in his baggage. One of his companions had said that he could buy a tiger's skin in Delhi, but the hunter said he preferred to get his own trophies.

These men had money to spend, and as most of the villagers needed money badly they were only too willing to go into the forest to construct a machan for the hunters. The platform, big enough to take the three men, was put up in the branches of a tall tun, or mahogany, tree.

It was the only night the hunters used the machan. At the end of March, though the days are warm, the nights are still cold. The hunters had neglected to bring blankets, and by midnight their teeth were chattering. Ramu, having tied up a buffalo calf for them at the foot of the tree, made as if to go home but instead circled the area, hanging up bits and pieces of old clothing on small trees and bushes. He thought he owed that much to the tiger. He knew the wily old king of the jungle would keep well away from the bait if he saw the bits of clothing—for where there were men's clothes, there would be men.

The vigil lasted well into the night but the tiger did not come near the tun tree. Perhaps he wasn't hungry; perhaps he got Ramu's message. In any case, the men in the tree soon gave themselves away.

The cold was really too much for them. A flask of rum was produced, and passed round, and it was not long before there was more purpose to finishing the rum than to finishing off a tiger. Silent at first, the men soon began talking in whispers; and to jungle creatures a human whisper is as telling as a trumpet call.

Soon the men were quite merry, talking in loud voices. And when the first morning light crept over the forest, and Ramu and his friends came back to fetch the great hunters, they found them fast asleep in the machan.

The hunters looked surly and embarrassed as they trudged back to the village.

'No game left in these parts,' said the American.

'Wrong time of the year for tiger,' said the second man.

'Don't know what the country's coming to,' said the third.

And complaining about the weather, the poor quality of cartridges, the quantity of rum they had drunk, and the perversity of tigers, they drove away in disgust.

It was not until the onset of summer that an event occurred which altered the hunting habits of the old tiger and brought him into conflict with the villagers.

There had been no rain for almost two months, and the tall jungle grass had become a sea of billowy dry yellow. Some refugee settlers, living in an area where the forest had been cleared, had been careless while cooking and had started a jungle fire. Slowly it spread into the interior, from where the acrid smell and the fumes smoked the tiger out towards the edge of the jungle. As night came on, the flames grew more vivid, and the smell stronger. The tiger turned and made for the jheel, where he knew he would be safe provided he swam across to the little island in the centre.

Next morning he was on the island, which was untouched

by the fire. But his surroundings had changed. The slopes of the hills were black with burnt grass, and most of the tall bamboo had disappeared. The deer and the wild pig, finding that their natural cover had gone, fled further east.

When the fire had died down and the smoke had cleared, the tiger prowled through the forest again but found no game. Once he came across the body of a burnt rabbit, but he could not eat it. He drank at the jheel and settled down in a shady spot to sleep the day away. Perhaps, by evening, some of the animals would return. If not, he, too, would have to look for new hunting grounds—or a new game.

The tiger spent five more days looking for a suitable game to kill. By that time he was so hungry that he even resorted to rooting among the dead leaves and burnt out stumps of trees, searching for worms and beetles. This was a sad comedown for the king of the jungle. But even now he hesitated to leave the area, for he had a deep suspicion and fear of the forest further east—forests that were fast being swallowed up by human habitation. He could have gone north, into high mountains, but they did not provide him with the long grass he needed. A panther could manage quite well up there, but not a tiger who loved the natural privacy of the heavy jungle. In the hills, he would have to hide all the time.

At daybreak, the tiger came to the jheel. The water was now shallow and muddy, and a green scum had spread over the top. But it was still drinkable and the tiger quenched his thirst.

He lay down across his favourite rock, hoping for a deer but none came. He was about to get up and go away when he heard an animal approach.

The tiger at once leaped off his perch and flattened himself on the ground, his tawny striped skin merging with the dry grass. A heavy animal was moving through the bushes, and the tiger waited patiently.

A buffalo emerged and came to the water.

The buffalo was alone.

He was a big male, and his long curved horns lay right back across his shoulders. He moved leisurely towards the water, completely unaware of the tiger's presence.

The tiger hesitated before making his charge. It was a long time—many years—since he had killed a buffalo, and he knew the villagers would not like it. But the pangs of hunger overcame his scruples. There was no morning breeze, everything was still, and the smell of the tiger did not reach the buffalo. A monkey chattered on a nearby tree, but his warning went unheeded.

Crawling stealthily on his stomach, the tiger skirted the edge of the jheel and approached the buffalo from the rear. The water birds, who were used to the presence of both animals, did not raise an alarm.

Getting closer, the tiger glanced around to see if there were men, or other buffaloes, in the vicinity. Then, satisfied that he was alone, he crept forward. The buffalo was drinking, standing in shallow water at the edge of the tank, when the tiger charged from the side and bit deep into the animal's thigh.

The buffalo turned to fight, but the tendons of his right hind leg had been snapped, and he could only stragger forward a few paces. But he was a buffalo—the bravest of the domestic cattle. He was not afraid. He snorted, and lowered his horns at the tiger; but the great cat was too fast, and circling the buffalo, bit into the other hind leg.

The buffalo crashed to the ground, both hind legs crippled, and then the tiger dashed in, using both tooth and claw, biting deep into the buffalo's throat until the blood gushed out from the jugular vein.

The buffalo gave one long, last bellow before dying.

The tiger, having rested, now began to gorge himself, but, even though he had been starving for days, he could not finish the huge carcass. At least one good meal still remained when, satisfied and feeling his strength returning, he quenched his thirst at the jheel. Then he dragged the remains of the buffalo into the bushes to hide it from the vultures, and went off to find a place to sleep.

He would return to the kill when he was hungry.

The villagers were upset when they discovered that a buffalo was missing; and the next day, when Ramu and Shyam came running home to say that they had found the carcass near the jheel, half-eaten by a tiger, the men were disturbed and angry. They felt that the tiger had tricked and deceived them. And they knew that once he got a taste for domestic cattle, he would make a habit of slaughtering them.

Kundan Singh, Shyam's father and the owner of the dead buffalo, said he would go after the tiger himself.

'It is all very well to talk about what you will do to the tiger,' said his wife, 'but you should never have let the buffalo go off on its own.'

'It had been out on his own before,' said Kundan. 'This is the first time the tiger has attacked one of our beasts. A devil must have entered the maharaja.'

'He must have been very hungry,' said Shyam.

'Well, we are hungry too,' said Kundan Singh.

'Our best buffalo—the only male in our herd.'

'The tiger will kill again,' said Ramu's father.

'If we let him,' said Kundan.

'Should we send for the shikaris?'

'No. They were not clever. The tiger will escape them easily. Besides, there is no time. The tiger will return for another meal tonight. We must finish him off ourselves!'

'But how?'

Kundan Singh smiled secretively, played with the ends of his moustache for a few moments, and then, with great pride, produced from under his cot a double-barrelled gun of ancient vintage.

'My father bought it from an Englishman,' he said.

'How long ago was that?'

'At the time I was born.'

'And have you ever used it?' asked Ramu's father, who was not sure that the gun would work.

'Well, some years back I let it off at some bandits. You remember the time when those dacoits raided our village? They chose the wrong village, and were severely beaten for their pains. As they left, I fired my gun off at them. They didn't stop running until they crossed the Ganga!'

'Yes, but did you hit anyone?'

'I would have, if someone's goat hadn't got in the way at the last moment. But we had roast mutton that night! Don't worry, brother, I know how the thing fires.'

Accompanied by Ramu's father and some others, Kundan set out for the jheel, where, without shifting the buffalo's carcass—for they knew that the tiger would not come near them if he suspected a trap—they made another machan in the branches of a tall tree some thirty feet from the kill.

Later that evening Kundan Singh and Ramu's father settled down for the night on their crude platform in the tree.

Several hours passed, and nothing but a jackal was seen by the watchers. And then, just as the moon came up over the distant hills, Kundan and his companion were startled by a low 'A-oonh', followed by a suppressed, rumbling growl.

Kundan grasped his old gun, whilst his friend drew closer to him for comfort. There was complete silence for a minute or two—time that was an agony of suspense for the watchers—and then the sound of stealthy footfalls on dead leaves under the trees.

A moment later the tiger walked out into the moonlight and stood over his kill.

At first Kundan could do nothing. He was completely overawed by the size of this magnificent tiger. Ramu's father had to nudge him, and then Kundan quickly put the gun to his shoulder, aimed at the tiger's head, and pressed the trigger.

The gun went off with a flash and two loud bangs, as Kundan fired both barrels. Then there was a tremendous roar. One of the bullets had grazed the tiger's head.

The enraged animal rushed at the tree and tried to leap up into the branches. Fortunately, the machan had been built at a safe height, and the tiger was unable to reach it. It roared again and then bounded off into the forest.

'What a tiger!' exclaimed Kundan, half in fear and half in admiration. 'I feel as though my liver has turned to water.'

'You missed him completely,' said Ramu's father. 'Your gun makes a big noise; an arrow would have done more damage.'

'I did not miss him,' said Kundan, feeling offended. 'You heard him roar, didn't you? Would he have been so angry if he had not been hit? If I have wounded him badly, he will die.'

'And if you have wounded him slightly, he may turn into a man-eater, and then where will we be?'

'I don't think he will come back,' said Kundan. 'He will leave these forests.'

They waited until the sun was up before coming down from the tree. They found a few drops of blood on the dry grass but no trail led into the forest, and Ramu's father was convinced that the wound was only a slight one.

The bullet, missing the fatal spot behind the ear, had only grazed the back of the skull and cut a deep groove at its base. It took a few days to heal, and during this time the tiger lay low and did not go near the jheel except when it was very dark and he was very thirsty.

The villagers thought the tiger had gone away, and Ramu and Shyam—accompanied by some other youths, and always carrying axes and lathis—began bringing buffaloes to the tank again during the day; but they were careful not to let any of them stray far from the herd, and they returned home while it was still daylight.

It was some days since the jungle had been ravaged by the fire, and in the tropics the damage is repaired quickly. In spite of it being the dry season, new life was creeping into the forest.

While the buffaloes wallowed in the muddy water, and the boys wrestled on their grassy islet, a big tawny eagle soared high above them, looking for a meal—a sure sign that some of the animals were beginning to return to the forest. It was not long before his keen eyes detected a movement in the glade below.

What the eagle with his powerful eyesight saw was a baby hare, a small fluffy thing, its long pink-tinted ears laid flat along its sides. Had it not been creeping along between two large stones, it would have escaped notice. The eagle waited to see if the mother was about, and as he waited he realized that he was not the only one who coveted this juicy morsel. From the bushes there had appeared a sinuous yellow creature, pressed low to the ground and moving rapidly towards the hare. It was a yellow jungle cat, hardly noticeable in the scorched grass. With great stealth the jungle cat began to stalk the baby hare.

He pounced. The hare's squeal was cut short by the cat's cruel claws; but it had been heard by the mother hare, who now bounded into the glade and without the slightest hesitation went for the surprised cat.

There was nothing haphazard about the mother hare's attack. She flashed around behind the cat and jumped clean over him. As she landed, she kicked back, sending a stinging jet of dust shooting into the cat's face. She did this again and again.

The bewildered cat, crouching and snarling, picked up the kill and tried to run away with it. But the hare would not permit this. She continued her leaping and buffeting, till eventually the cat, out of sheer frustration, dropped the kill and attacked the mother.

The cat sprang at the hare a score of times, lashing out with his claws; but the mother hare was both clever and agile enough to keep just out of reach of those terrible claws, and drew the cat further and further away from her baby—for she did not as yet know that it was dead.

The tawny eagle saw his chance. Swift and true, he swooped. For a brief moment, as his wings overspread the furry little hare and his talons sank deep into it, he caught a glimpse of the cat racing towards him and the mother hare fleeing into the bushes. And then with a shrill 'kee-ee-ee' of triumph, he rose and whirled away with his dinner.

The boys had heard his shrill cry and looked up just in time to see the eagle flying over the jheel with the small little hare held firmly in his talons.

'Poor hare,' said Shyam. 'Its life was short.'

'That's the law of the jungle,' said Ramu. 'The eagle has

a family, too, and must feed it.'

'I wonder if we are any better than animals,' said Shyam.

'Perhaps we are a little better, in some ways,' said Ramu. 'Grandfather always says, "To be able to laugh and to be merciful are the only things that make man better than the beast."'

The next day, while the boys were taking the herd home, one of the buffaloes lagged behind. Ramu did not realize that the animal was missing until he heard an agonized bellow behind him. He glanced over his shoulder just in time to see the big striped tiger dragging the buffalo into a clump of young bamboo. At the same time the herd became aware of the danger, and the buffaloes snorted with fear as they hurried along the forest path. To urge them forward, and to warn his friends, Ramu cupped his hands to his mouth and gave vent to a yodelling call.

The buffaloes bellowed, the boys shouted, and the birds flew shrieking from the trees. It was almost a stampede by the time the herd emerged from the forest. The villagers heard the thunder of hoofs, and saw the herd coming home amidst clouds of dust and confusion, and knew that something was wrong.

'The tiger!' shouted Ramu. 'He is here! He has killed one of the buffaloes.'

'He is afraid of us no longer,' said Shyam.

'Did you see where he went?' asked Kundan Singh, hurrying up to them.

'I remember the place,' said Ramu. 'He dragged the buffalo in amongst the bamboo.'

'Then there is no time to lose,' said his father. 'Kundan, you take your gun and two men, and wait near the suspension bridge, where the Garur stream joins the Ganga. The jungle is narrow there. We will beat the jungle from our side, and drive the tiger towards you. He will not escape us, unless he swims the river!'

'Good!' said Kundan, running into his house for his gun, with Shyam close at his heels. 'Was it one of our buffaloes again?' he asked.

'It was Ramu's buffalo this time,' said Shyam. 'A good milk buffalo.'

'Then Ramu's father will beat the jungle thoroughly. You boys had better come with me. It will not be safe for you to accompany the beaters.'

Kundan Singh, carrying his gun and accompanied by Ramu, Shyam and two men, headed for the river junction, while Ramu's father collected about twenty men from the village and, guided by one of the boys who had been with Ramu, made for the spot where the tiger had killed the buffalo.

The tiger was still eating when he heard the men coming. He had not expected to be disturbed so soon. With an angry 'Whoof!' he bounded into a bamboo thicket and watched the men through a screen of leaves and tall grass.

The men did not seem to take much notice of the dead buffalo, but gathered round their leader and held a consultation. Most of them carried hand drums slung from their shoulders. They also carried sticks, spears and axes.

After a hurried conversation, they entered the denser part of the jungle, beating their drums with the palms of their hands. Some of the men banged empty kerosene tins. These made even more noise than the drums.

The tiger did not like the noise and retreated deeper into the jungle. But he was surprised to find that the men, instead of going away, came after him into the jungle, banging away on their drums and tins, and shouting at the top of their voices. They had separated now, and advanced single or in pairs, but nowhere were they more than fifteen yards apart. The tiger could easily have broken through this slowly advancing semicircle of men—one swift blow from his paw would have felled the strongest of them—but his main aim was to get away from the noise. He hated and feared noise made by men.

He was not a man-eater and he would not attack a man unless he was very angry or frightened or very desperate; and he was none of these things as yet. He had eaten well, and he would have liked to rest in peace—but there would be no rest for any animal until the men ceased their tremendous clatter and din.

For an hour Ramu's father and others beat the jungle, calling, drumming and trampling the undergrowth. The tiger had no rest. Whenever he was able to put some distance between himself and the men, he would sink down in some shady spot to rest; but, within five or ten minutes, the trampling and drumming would sound nearer, and the tiger, with an angry snarl, would get up and pad north, pad silently north along the narrowing strip of jungle, towards the junction of the Garur stream and the Ganga. Ten years back, he would have had the jungle on his right in which to hide; but the trees had been felled long ago to make way for humans and houses, and now he could only move to the left, towards the river.

It was about noon when the tiger finally appeared in the open. He longed for the darkness and security of the night, for the sun was his enemy. Kundan and the boys had a clear view of him as he stalked slowly along, now in the open with the sun glinting on his glossy hide, now in the shade or passing through the shorter reeds. He was still out of range of Kundan's gun, but there was no fear of his getting out of the beat, as the 'stops' were all picked men from the village. He disappeared among some bushes but soon reappeared to retrace his steps, the beaters having done their work well. He was now only 150 yards from the rocks where Kundan Singh waited, and he looked very big.

The beat had closed in, and the exit along the bank downstream was completely blocked, so the tiger turned and disappeared into a belt of reeds, and Kundan Singh expected that the head would soon peer out of the cover a few yards away. The beaters were row making a great noise, shouting and beating their drums, but nothing moved; and Ramu, watching from a distance, wondered, 'Has he slipped through the beaters?' And he half-hoped so.

Tins clashed, drums beat, and some of the men poked into the reeds with their spears or long bamboos. Perhaps one of these thrusts found a mark, because at last the tiger was roused, and with an angry desperate snarl he charged out of the reeds, splashing his way through an inlet of mud and water.

Kundan Singh fired, and his bullet struck the tiger on the thigh.

The mighty animal stumbled; but he was up in a minute, and rushing through a gap in the narrowing line of beaters, he made straight for the only way across the river—the suspension bridge that passed over the Ganga here, providing a route into the high hills beyond.

'We'll get him now,' said Kundan, priming his gun again. 'He's right in the open!'

The suspension bridge swayed and trembled as the wounded tiger lurched across it. Kundan fired, and this time the bullet grazed the tiger's shoulder. The animal bounded forward, lost his footing on the unfamiliar, slippery planks of the swaying bridge, and went over the side, falling headlong into the strong, swirling waters of the river.

He rose to the surface once, but the current took him under and away, and only a thin streak of blood remained on the river's surface.

Kundan and others hurried downstream to see if the dead tiger had been washed up on the river's banks; but though they searched the riverside several miles, they did not find the king of the forest.

He had not provided anyone with a trophy. His skin would not be spread on a couch, nor would his head be hung up on a wall. No claw of his would be hung as a charm round the neck of a child. No villager would use his fat as a cure for rheumatism.

At first the villagers were glad because they felt their buffaloes were safe. Then the men began to feel that something had gone out of their lives, out of the life of the forest; they began to feel that the forest was no longer a forest. It had been shrinking year by year, but, as long as the tiger had been there and the villagers had heard it roar at night, they had known that they were still secure from the intruders and newcomers who came to fell the trees and eat up the land and let the flood waters into the village. But now that the tiger had gone, it was as though a protector had gone, leaving the forest open and vulnerable, easily destroyable. And once the forest was destroyed they, too, would be in danger…

There was another thing that had gone with the tiger, another thing that had been lost, a thing that was being lost everywhere—something called 'nobility'.

Ramu remembered something that his grandfather had once said, 'The tiger is the very soul of India, and when the last tiger goes, so will the soul of the country.'

The boys lay flat on their stomachs on their little mud island and watched the monsoon clouds gathering overhead.

'The king of our forest is dead,' said Shyam. 'There are no more tigers.'

'There must be tigers,' said Ramu. 'How can there be an India without tigers?'

The river had carried the tiger many miles away from his home, from the forest he had always known, and brought him ashore on a strip of warm yellow sand, where he lay in the sun, quite still, but breathing.

Vultures gathered and waited at a distance, some of them perching on the branches of nearby trees.

But the tiger was more drowned than hurt, and as the river water oozed out of his mouth, and the warm sun made new life throb through his body, he stirred and stretched, and his glazed eyes came into focus. Raising his head, he saw trees and tall grass.

Slowly he heaved himself off the ground and moved at a crouch to where the grass waved in the afternoon breeze. Would he be harried again, and shot at? There was no smell of man. The tiger moved forward with greater confidence.

There was, however, another smell in the air—a smell that reached back to the time when he was young and fresh and full of vigour—a smell that he had almost forgotten but could never quite forget—the smell of a tigress!

He raised his head high, and new life surged through his tired limbs. He gave a full-throated roar and moved purposefully through the tall grass. And the roar came back to him, calling him, calling him forward—a roar that meant there would be more tigers in the land!

THE PALE ONE

John Eyton

I

The Pale One was one of the most mysterious creatures in the world a she-elephant, queen of her herd and of the vast jungles wherein they moved. Her kingdom stretched from the blue Nilgiri Hills, through leagues of rugged hillocks clothed in scrub, to the dense jungles on the Cauvery's banks. She and her kind had but little to do with the works of man, save for the occasional descent on a village at the jungle edge, when they would maraud a few fields for fodder; sometimes too in the dusk, on the Ootacamund road or on the way to Mercara, men would see great shadowy forms ahead of them, and would flee—but she was hardly aware of man at all.

Perhaps, her colour had attracted the great Tusker, who had wandered alone in the forests of Coorg until a bullet drove him from his old haunts into the jungle by the river. One evening, he saw the herd at drinking, and challenged at once, stamping and roaring and calling their ancient leader—the giant of the One Tusk—to battle; then all night he wandered round the bamboo brake, trumpeting defiance. In the morning the memorable battle started, which lasted three days and determined, in sight of all, the leadership of the herd. The jungle-folk kept away; even the tiger and the buffalo avoided the battle-ground, where trees were uprooted and pounded into the floor; where the very forest swayed to the movements of the fighters, while the cows trembled for their calves, and the young males stood aloof and envied the prowess. At last, height and great spirit won the victory over age and experience; the elephant of the One Tusk went alone and wounded from his kingdom, never to be seen again, while the great black Tusker danced the dance of victory and lorded it over the young males, and chose his bride.

She was of a paler grey than the rest, who were almost black, and her paleness came of an old stock, and won her his regard. So, the Pale One knew her lord.

Who can tell of the wanderings of the herd during the three years which followed? They rarely stayed long in one place. In the rainy time they sought the hills, and in the dry time they followed the river, where they would stand at evening in the deep, draining great gulps, squirting one another, teaching the young to swim, revelling in the cool and depth of it. Great, black, shiny monsters they were, but by the side of the greatest of all was always one of paler hue, whom he served, towering over her with his immense height, full of tusk, broad of forehead, with great spreading ears. He ruled the twenty-five elephants of the herd sternly, nor brooked interference from other herds which crossed their path, so that they became famous, and had the freedom of all the jungles of the south, with the coolest places for the heat, the best drinking pools, and the sweetest bamboo groves. No elephant ever stood in the path of the big black Tusker, lord of the Pale One.

In the third summer of their wandering, directly after the rains, there came a spirit of unrest on the herd. They were leaving the hills for the country of green scrub and luscious fresh food, welcoming the sun, which they had not seen for many days. Yet, one day, as they stood basking in the open, a feeling of restlessness came on them. To an elephant this means either that he is in love or that he is being interfered with; in the latter case it is the instinct of the curtailment of that freedom which is his birthright. The old mother of the herd felt it first, as it came on the breeze to her, and she communicated the news. They were not alone in the jungle; something was stirring between them and the hills—other elephants perhaps—or something unknown.

One or two of the younger males threw up their trunks and squealed, and were promptly dealt with by the Tusker, who wanted to listen, and said so; then shuffling and stamping ceased; mothers quieted their calves; only the breeze from the hills sighed in the grass and tiny birds twittered; then from far away knowledge came to them.

The ground vibrated ever so slightly; other elephants were afoot...a great herd...two, three herds...one from the direction of the sun, another from the hills, and another from the plain of great grass. But there was something else...a new smell, vaguely disconcerting...men.

Then, an unusual thing happened; the big Tusker did not, as was his wont, turn to challenge the new herds but began to move uneasily, aloof from the rest, throwing his trunk and shifting his feet; presently he moved slowly away, and the Pale One joined him; then, one by one, the rest followed. When they were together, the rush quickened to full pace, and they thrust through the thickets, massed like a wedge, driving a road over the country, never stopping till nightfall. It was a new experience—the first of many—and it meant panic. The herd had rarely travelled like that, at full pace, *en masse*, careless of its mothers and the calves...and never for a whole day. But they got beyond the area of unrest, and were in free land again, where the ground brought no vibrations, and the breeze no upsetting smell. They did not forget these things, because only a few things are forgotten by elephants, but they puzzled over them that night, and next day moved on towards the distant river jungles, not en masse; but in open feeding formation, eating as they went. For two days they travelled on over the low hillocks, each day making a longer midday halt; then, on the third day, they came upon a little pool with good green feeding on its banks, where they stayed a night and a day, carelessly feeding and wallowing. But at dusk they saw a new thing.

The older ones had seen it before, and thought little of it at a distance if they were hungry. What they saw was a line of little points of light, flashing out behind them, like stars over the hill; the wind brought smoke too, which tickled the trunk curiously; and there were little sounds, such as they had heard in villages; then a faint sound which they knew well—the far-off call of a she-elephant—the night call. Familiar it was, and yet unfamiliar; it brought back the spirit of unrest to them, for it was not a free call—it had trouble in it, such as they did not understand.

At the second trumpeting, the herd left the sucking mud and plunged into the darkness, careless of what they trampled or where they went, driving in fear through the night. From that time they knew restless days and nights; the sense of freedom had passed.

II

The twinkling lights were not those of a village, but of a great camp.

There were a hundred campfires on the side of a low hill, and around them many men squatted. The red glow lit up wild faces among the little tents and the trees; there was bustle of cooking and a good smell of hot food; pipes were being passed around from mouth to mouth, and in every group there was one who talked of elephants, and many who nodded. Here were grizzled old mahouts, heroes of many kheddahs,[1] who spoke of great elephants as if they were children, and wore the Maharajah's medals; their sons, smooth-faced young men in bright turbans, who hung upon their words; the elephant servants—thin, bearded Mohammedans, with sleepy, drugged eyes; the trackers—wild, hairy jungle men, almost naked, talking in strange tongues; and, besides, a motley crew of beaters and chamars[2] and water-carriers and coolies from Mysore and Malabar, who raised a babel of chatter. The only restful things were the lines of dim elephants in the background, silent for the most part, save when one trumpeted or brushed a branch to and fro with his trunk to clear it of dust. The fire flickers just showed these swaying forms under the trees, dignified amid the bustle, eating unhurriedly their heaps of green branches.

Meals were eaten; from some of the groups came snatches of song—the crooning of Southern love, and the triumphs of roping elephants; a drum was beaten in the shadows; then the talk died and men lay down, muffled in brown blankets, while

---

[1] Kheddah: Enclosure.
[2] Chamar: Tanner, leather-worker

the watchers sat silent. At last, there was no sound but the shuffling and munching of the great sentinels of the moving camp, the driving elephants of Mysore.

There was, indeed, good cause for the panic of the wild herd. That moving camp was full of purpose, and the khaki-clad man with the eyes of a hunter, who ruled it, knew his business. This was the central camp of three, moving in the form of crescent over the elephant country, tracking herds, and persuading them gently forward day-by-day in the direction of the Cauvery Kheddahs. At present they were rounding up, but their most difficult duty lay ahead, and began with the exact timing of the last drive at close quarters when the three groups should converge on the same day. But it was all hard work, for they were moving in country untouched by man, far from villages and crops—the country of wild elephant and buffalo. Their strange encounters in thicket and by river while driving or fetching chara[3] would fill many stories; but they were travelling all the time, tracking as they went, keeping touch with the other groups in a land of no communications, and rounding up stray elephants from the wild herds.

They had made touch with three herds in all, and the biggest was in the middle. Only one man had seen this herd, which had moved forward like a phantom at full pace, and he spoke of a giant, a rajah among elephants, and of a pale tuskless elephant, standing out of the welter of the rest; the mighty mallan,[4] the torn-up trees, and the scarred tree-trunks on the elephant path showed that he spoke the truth, and that this was the master herd. By the time the three camps had converged in

---

[3]Chara: Feed of elephants.
[4]Mallan: Track of an elephant.

the neighbourhood of Karapur, where deep jungle flanks the Cauvery River, the Pale One and her lord had become famous, almost legendary...the theme of many a mahout's prayer and triumph-song. The herd had the reputation of being restless; as it was feared that they might overshoot the kheddah jungle and cross the river, they had not been over harried or molested. On the night before the kheddah drive they were tearing the bamboo near the river's edge, uneasy, but settled for the time being. There was a great suspense in the camp of two thousand men and two hundred elephants, gathered for the final act of their long drama.

III

Ever since the stampede from the pool the wild herd had travelled fast—too fast for the Pale One, who was shortly destined to present her lord with a son. More and more she had lagged behind, and only a great heart had helped her through. So, when at last they reached the welcome shade of the river jungle she lay down and rested long, while the others were tearing at the trees and rejoicing at having thrown off the unrest.

But they rejoiced too soon, for on the third day, as they were moving for the evening drink, they heard the trumpeting of an elephant near at hand, again and again, whereat the big Tusker stopped to listen, flapping his ears and gently raising his trunk. There were elephants close behind them...but not only elephants—there were men, many men. Sounds of drums and gongs and stirring and shouting filtered the trees as the herd fidgeted uneasily and began to mass. There was a moment of uncertainty, and then they saw lights in the wood, waving and bobbing, and waited to see no more; they crashed forward, shambling through the dense growth till they came out on to the sand by the river, where the red rays of the setting sun lit up the water and intensified the gloom of the farther bank...then they plunged into the stream, the great Tusker leading and the Pale One in the rear, and between them a surge of scrambling subjects, old and young, half-grown and calves, fighting to gain the gloom of the bank beyond.

Then, suddenly that gloom burst into flame. Even the unconquerable drive of a wild herd was pulled up short. One moment all had been darkness and silence ahead of them; the next, men burst from the trees in hundreds with shouts and sudden noises like the rending of trees—and, above all, the lights. They could not face those torches. Dazed, bewildered, they turned upstream, to find that elephants had put into the water from both banks and were advancing in line; the bank which they had left, too, was full of dancing, leaping men with lights. The herd hesitated; two young males broke away upstream and flung themselves against the line: It was like dashing against a brick wall. They met four great old Tuskers, who pushed them squealing downstream with ugly blows in the ribs, while sharp spears pricked them in tender places from above, and loud cracks rang in their ears; smarting, buffeted, stunned, they blundered into the deep water with a gurgle and a splash, and half-swam, half-floundered past the herd, which was standing at bay. A black mass they made against the red sky-the humped forms gathered round the big Tusker, who with angry eyes, ears out, trunk extended, awaited the first shock.

Then, with a rush and a bump, the line met them; there was a mighty swaying and pushing—loud gun-shots, flashes, sharp thrusts, cries of men, smell of gunpowder—all in a melee; but the advancing line had the advantage of science, impetus, and the stream, and the wild herd had to give, breaking and scattering suddenly, the Pale One leading the rout. It was not her way to flee, but she knew that she must reserve her strength and trust her lord.

So the herd broke, but their spirit was not gone. Amid pandemonium from both banks there were a dozen individual fights as elephant after elephant broke back, leaving only the mothers with their calves to take their time and move on; but, one-by-one, they encountered new tactics, for they were cut off, roughly hustled, and mastered in detail, fight as they would. The big Tusker, who held the rear, found himself the special charge of four full-grown elephants; he could have tackled the lot in the open, unhampered, but here he was too angry for strategy; when he knocked one out of his way the other three butted into him from behind; and when he turned to vent his wrath he saw flashes and had stinging pains in the head. So, he could but lash and storm and ramp like a half-grown elephant, sending up the water in great sprays around him, as he was gradually edged down below the steep right bank in the wake of the rest.

So, the herd was passing down the river, when suddenly the Pale One stood still. Below her, stretched across the stream, she saw another line—silent, impassive, motionless—of full forty elephants. She looked right and left; on the left the crowd still surged with their torches; on the right was the high bank—but here was a gap in the bank and a track into dark jungle above. Slowly and uncertainly she made for that gap, still suspicious, but, as nothing happened, she walked up the track, past a fence, into a bamboo grove. Then the herd, bundled together between two converging lines, massed again and followed their queen; last of all came the big Tusker, who stood proudly at bay in the middle of the gap. Then, a whole constellation of flashes dazed his eyes, and he, the lord of the Southern jungles, turned and followed his herd. Something clashed behind him—timber on timber. They were in kheddah.

IV

It was as if they had passed through a nightmare, and had awakened in good feeding jungle and absolute quiet. True, there were fires round the circle of the bamboo patch, and a jumble of sound, but they were not molested. The younger elephants started at once to feed on the bamboo, but the great Tusker remained aloof and sulky, touring round the patch and trying the defences. He found that they were surrounded by a ditch that could not be crossed and a timber fence that could not be reached, and his defiant trumpeting woke the echoes and told the herd that all was not well.

But the Pale One was beyond caring, for her time was very near. That night she went apart from the rest, and in the morning there lay beside her a little crumpled grey object no bigger than a sheep-dog. In the dim morning she stood over it, and caressed it with her trunk, till soon it tottered to its feet, and felt for her; so she fed it, forgetting the nightmare for a while.

For a day and a night they had peace, and she grew to love her little one at her side, playing with it, feeling all over it with her trunk, giving her milk freely for its strength, watching it find its feet.

Then, on the morning of the second day, the nightmare returned. The great Tusker, in his pilgrimage round the ditch, suddenly came face-to-face with a line of elephants drawn up outside for battle; he parted the bamboos, and for a long time remained gazing, measuring, taking stock...then slowly turned and rejoined the herd. Then they heard the opening of the gates and the entry of the enemy...so the great fight began.

They had good hope this time; they had rested and were in the open—their own ground; and they were prepared. The Pale One went at once to a lonely corner, her little one ambling along at her side, while her lord led the charge in mass formation at the centre of the line. But, as they closed, the noises started again, and the pricks in tender parts, and all the bewilderments of the first fight. Once more they encountered science that was not of the wild, for they were deftly cut up and hustled in batches in the direction of a tall enclosure with a narrow entrance. Soon, it became evident that the strangers meant to drive them into that enclosure, and they resisted with might and main, breaking back again and again, scattering the enemy, they rallying to their leader...but always the enemy re-formed and encircled them. At noon honours were still equal, for the enemy retired outside, while the herd made for a muddy little swamp with shallow water in it, and for an hour drank deep for refreshment, and blew out spouts of muddy water to cool one another. Only the Pale One did not join them, tending her babe apart, ill at ease.

When the fight began again, the enemy had reinforced; the herd was completely surrounded in the swamp, and hustled pell-mell towards the enclosure, where a last stand was made against overwhelming numbers; nothing availed: willy-nilly they were bundled through the gap into the small enclosure, where they heaved and barged and squeezed, trumpeting and squealing, making the timbers creak.

Only the great Tusker managed to break away, irresistibly, as a ship drives through water, sending three elephants headlong before him. He stood near the gate, gathering his strength for an ugly rush, ready to take on the whole line in fair fight...

But the fight was not fair; as he was advancing, there came the last indignity, and the first knowledge of slavery...the rope touched him. Deftly his head was lassoed; then a hind leg; then another; then came a mad struggle against six elephants tugging at the end of the ropes; he became aware of men too, and struggled the more. The old freedom had gone; he could not fight devilry-creepers that twined and would not break. Dimly understanding that his hour had come, and that his birthright had been stolen from him, he suffered himself to be drawn away by the six down a steep bank into the cooling river...out of sight of his herd.

So passed the great Tusker into the haunts of men for the years of slavery.

It was the Pale One who made the Homeric fight, which will be told over campfires a generation hence. They found her in a corner, tending her babe, and she confronted them, pushing the babe beneath her body. Then they hemmed her in, but the trained elephants shrank from her and would not close, for all that she was the smaller and alone. Men said afterwards that she was bewitched, for she made the boldest half-hearted, and drove through them, butting with her broad forehead, striking with her heavy trunk. For an hour she led the hunt, and they could not catch her nor close with her; even when defeat seemed certain she broke the line with the force of a ram, and the boldest turned from her. She was fighting for more than life, or the honour of the herd, or the freedom of the South: she was battling for her young, and dimly she knew what the loss of the fight would mean—the loss of the love she felt for him.

She never would have been taken alive had she not looked down and missed her babe...saw it being led away...gave a mad squeal, and chased, with destruction in her eyes...then thundered against the great gates of the palisade.

So at last, they caught her easily enough. The Pale One had nothing more to fight for.

In the evening she stood alone under a tall tree, the chain clanking at her leg. While the others trumpeted and fought their chains, she was silent, with an ineffable sadness. Pale and ghostly she loomed against the glow of the campfires, and men watched and wondered at her. Then, they brought her the little grey elephant-babe, which ran up to her and commanded milk with its tiny trunk...

The Pale One turned her head slowly away. The free days were past, and she would never know her babe again.

THE LEOPARD

Ruskin Bond

I first saw the leopard when I was crossing the small stream at the bottom of the hill.

The ravine was so deep that for most of the day it remained in shadow. This encouraged many birds and animals to emerge from cover during the daylight hours. Few people ever passed that way: only milkmen and charcoal burners from the surrounding villages. As a result, the ravine had become a little haven for wildlife, one of the few natural sanctuaries left near Mussoorie, a hill station in northern India.

Below my cottage was a forest of oak and maple and Himalayan rhododendron. A narrow path twisted its way down through the trees, over an open ridge where red sorrel grew wild, and then steeply down through a tangle of wild raspberries, creeping vines and slender bamboo. At the bottom of the hill the path led on to a grassy verge, surrounded by wild dog roses. (It is surprising how closely the flora of the lower Himalayas, between 5,000 and 8,000 feet, resembles that of the English countryside.)

The stream ran close by the verge, tumbling over smooth

pebbles, over rocks worn yellow with age, on its way to the plains and to the little Song River and finally to the sacred Ganga River.

When I first discovered the stream, it was early April and the wild roses were flowering—small white blossoms lying in clusters.

I walked down to the stream almost every day after two or three hours of writing. I had lived in cities too long and had returned to the hills to renew myself, both physically and mentally. Once you have lived with mountains for any length of time you belong to them, and must return again and again.

Nearly every morning, and sometimes during the day, I heard the cry of the barking deer. And in the evening, walking through the forest, I disturbed parties of pheasants. The birds went gliding down the ravine on open, motionless wings. I saw pine martens and a handsome red fox, and I recognized the footprints of a bear.

As I had not come to take anything from the forest, the birds and animals soon grew accustomed to my presence; or possibly they recognized my footsteps. After some time, my approach did not disturb them.

The langoors in the oak and rhododendron trees, who would at first go leaping through the branches at my approach, now watched me with some curiosity as they munched the tender green shoots of the oak. The young ones scuffled and wrestled like boys while their parents groomed each other's coats, stretching themselves out on the sunlit hillside.

But one evening, as I passed, I heard them chattering in the trees, and I knew I was not the cause of their excitement. As I crossed the stream and began climbing the hill, the grunting and chattering increased, as though the langoors were trying to warn me of some hidden danger. A shower of pebbles came rattling down the steep hillside, and I looked up to see a sinewy, orange-gold leopard poised on a rock about twenty feet above me.

He was not looking towards me but had his head thrust attentively forward, in the direction of the ravine. Yet he must have sensed my presence, because, he slowly turned his head and looked down at me.

He seemed a little puzzled at my presence there; and when, to give myself courage, I clapped my hands sharply, the leopard sprang away into the thickets, making absolutely no sound as he melted into the shadows.

I had disturbed the animal in his quest for food. But a little after I heard the quickening cry of a barking deer as it fled through the forest. The hunt was still on.

The leopard, like other members of the cat family, is nearing extinction in India, and I was surprised to find one so close to Mussoorie. Probably the deforestation that had been taking place in the surrounding hills had driven the deer into this green valley; and the leopard, naturally, had followed.

It was some weeks before I saw the leopard again, although I was often made aware of its presence. A dry, rasping cough sometimes gave it away. At times I felt almost certain that I was being followed.

Once, when I was late getting home, and the brief twilight gave way to a dark moonless night, I was startled by a family of porcupines running about in a clearing. I looked around nervously and saw two bright eyes staring at me from a thicket. I stood still, my heart banging away against my ribs. Then the eyes danced away and I realized that they were only fireflies.

In May and June, when the hills are brown and dry, it

is always cool and green near the stream, where ferns and maidenhair and long grasses continue to thrive.

Downstream I found a small pool where I could bathe, and a cave with water dripping from the roof, the water spangled gold and silver in the shafts of sunlight that pushed through the slits in the cave roof.

'He maketh me to lie down in green pastures; he leadeth me beside the still waters.' Perhaps David had discovered a similar paradise when he wrote those words; perhaps I, too, would write good words. The hill station's summer visitors had not discovered this haven of wild and green things. I was beginning to feel that the place belonged to me, that dominion was mine.

The stream had at least one other regular visitor, a spotted forktail, and though it did not fly away at my approach, it became restless if I stayed too long, and then she would move from boulder to boulder uttering a long complaining cry.

I spent an afternoon trying to discover the bird's nest, which I was certain contained young ones, because I had seen the forktail carrying grubs in her bill. The problem was that when the bird flew upstream, I had difficulty in following her rapidly enough as the rocks were sharp and slippery.

Eventually I decorated myself with bracken fronds and, after slowly making my way upstream, hid myself in the hollow stump of a tree at a spot where the forktail often disappeared. I had no intention of robbing the bird. I was simply curious to see its home.

By crouching down, I was able to command a view of a small stretch of the stream and the side of the ravine; but I had done little to deceive the forktail, who continued to object strongly to my presence so near her home.

I summoned up my reserves of patience and sat perfectly

still for about ten minutes. The forktail quietened down. Out of sight, out of mind. But where had she gone? Probably into the walls of the ravine where, I felt sure, she was guarding her nest.

I decided to take her by surprise and stood up suddenly, in time to see not the forktail on her doorstep but the leopard bounding away with a grunt of surprise! Two urgent springs, and he had crossed the stream and plunged into the forest.

I was as astonished as the leopard, and forgot all about the forktail and her nest. Had the leopard been following me again?

I decided against this possibility. Only man-eaters follow humans and, as far as I knew, there had never been a man-eater in the vicinity of Mussoorie.

During the monsoon the stream became a rushing torrent; bushes and small trees were swept away, and the friendly murmur of the water became a threatening boom. I did not visit the place too often as there were leeches in the long grass.

One day I found the remains of a barking deer, which had only been partly eaten. I wondered why the leopard had not hidden the rest of his meal, and decided that it must have been disturbed while eating.

Then, climbing the hill, I met a party of hunters resting beneath the oaks. They asked me if I had seen a leopard. I said I had not. They said they knew there was a leopard in the forest.

Leopard skins, they told me, were selling in Delhi at over a thousand rupees each. Of course there was a ban on the export of skins, but they gave me to understand that there were ways and means... I thanked them for their information and walked on, feeling uneasy and disturbed.

The hunters had seen the carcass of the deer, and they had seen the leopard's pug marks, and they kept coming to the forest. Almost every evening I heard their guns banging away;

for they were ready to fire at almost anything.

'There's a leopard about,' they always told me.

'You should carry a gun.'

'I don't have one,' I said.

There were fewer birds to be seen, and even the langoors had moved on. The red fox did not show itself; and the pine martens, who had become quite bold, now dashed into hiding at my approach. The smell of one human is like the smell of any other.

And then the rains were over and it was October. I could lie in the sun, on sweet-smelling grass, and gaze up through a pattern of oak leaves into a blinding blue heaven. And I would praise God for leaves and grass and the smell of things—the smell of mint and bruised clover—and the touch of things—the touch of grass and air and sky, the touch of the sky's blueness.

I thought no more of the men. My attitude towards them was similar to that of the denizens of the forest. These were men, unpredictable, and to be avoided if possible.

On the other side of the ravine rose Pari Tibba, Hill of the Fairies; a bleak, scrub-covered hill where no one lived.

It was said that in the previous century Englishmen had tried building their houses on the hill, but the area had always attracted lightning, due to either the hill's location or due to its mineral deposits; after several houses had been struck by lighting, the settlers had moved on to the next hill, where the town now stands.

To the hillmen it is Pari Tibba, haunted by the spirits of a pair of ill-fated lovers who perished there in a storm; to others it is known as Burnt Hill, because of its scarred and stunted trees.

One day, after crossing the stream, I climbed Pari Tibba—a stiff undertaking, because there was no path to the top and I had to scramble up a precipitous rock face with the help of rocks and roots that were apt to come loose in my groping hand.

But at the top was a plateau with a few pine trees, their upper branches catching the wind and humming softly. There I found the ruins of what must have been the houses of the first settlers—just a few piles of rubble, now overgrown with weeds, sorrel, dandelions and nettles.

As I walked though the roofless ruins, I was struck by the silence that surrounded me, the absence of birds and animals, the sense of complete desolation.

The silence was so absolute that it seemed to be ringing in my ears. But there was something else of which I was becoming increasingly aware: The strong feline odour of one of the cat family. I paused and looked about. I was alone. There was no movement of dry leaf or loose stone.

The ruins were for the most part open to the sky. Their rotting rafters had collapsed, jamming together to form a low passage like the entrance to a mine; and this dark cavern seemed to lead down into the ground. The smell was stronger when I approached this spot, so I stopped again and waited there, wondering if I had discovered the lair of the leopard, wondering if the animal was now at rest after a night's hunt.

Perhaps he was crouching there in the dark, watching me, recognizing me, knowing me as the man who walked alone in the forest without a weapon.

I like to think that he was there, that he knew me, and that he acknowledged my visit in the friendliest way: by ignoring me altogether.

Perhaps I had made him confident—too confident, too careless, too trusting of the human in his midst. I did not venture any further; I was not out of my mind. I did not seek physical contact, or even another glimpse of that beautiful sinewy body, springing from rock to rock. It was his trust I wanted, and I think he gave it to me.

But did the leopard, trusting one man, make the mistake of bestowing his trust on others? Did I, by casting out all fear—my own fear, and the leopard's protective fear—leave him defenceless? Because the next day, coming up the path from the stream, shouting and beating drums, were the hunters. They had a long bamboo pole across their shoulders; and slung from the pole, feet up, head down, was the lifeless body of the leopard, shot in the neck and in the head.

'We told you there was a leopard!' they shouted, in great good humour. 'Isn't he a fine specimen?'

'Yes,' I said. 'He was a beautiful leopard.'

I walked home through the silent forest. It was very silent, almost as though the birds and animals knew that their trust had been violated.

I remembered the lines of a poem by D.H. Lawrence; and, as I climbed the steep and lonely path to my home, the words beat out their rhythm in my mind: 'There was room in the world for a mountain lion and me.'

CAULFIELD'S CRIME

Alice Perrin

Caulfield was a sulky, bad-tempered individual who made no friends and was deservedly unpopular, but he had the reputation of being the finest shot in the Punjab, and of possessing a knowledge of sporting matters that was almost superhuman. He was an extremely jealous shot, and hardly ever invited a companion to join him on his shooting trips, so it may be understood that I was keenly alive to the honour conferred on me when he suddenly asked me to go out for three days' small game shooting with him.

'I know a string of jheels,' he said, 'about thirty miles from here, where the duck and snipe must swarm. I marked the place down when I was out last month, and I've made arrangements to go there next Friday morning. You can come, too, if you like.'

I readily accepted the ungracious invitation, though I could hardly account for it, knowing his solitary ways, except that he probably thought that I was unlikely to assert myself, being but a youngster, and also he knew me better than he did most people, for our houses were next door, and I often strolled over to examine his enormous collection of skins and horns and other sporting trophies.

I bragged about the coming expedition in the club that evening, and was well-snubbed by two or three men who would have given anything to know the whereabouts of Caulfield's string of jheels, and who spitefully warned me to be careful that Caulfield did not end by shooting me.

'I believe he'd kill any chap who annoyed him,' said one of them, looking round to make sure that Caulfield was not at hand. 'I never met such a nasty-tempered fellow, I believe he's mad. But he can shoot, and what he doesn't know about game isn't worth knowing.'

Caulfield and I rode out the thirty miles early on the Friday morning, having sent our camp on ahead the previous night. We found our tents pitched in the scanty shade of some stunted dak jungle trees with thick dry bark, flat, shapeless leaves, that clattered together when stirred by the wind, and wicked-looking red blossoms. It was not a cheerful spot, and the soil was largely mixed with salt which had worked its way in white patches to the surface, and only encouraged the growth of the rankest of grass.

Before us stretched a dreary outlook of shallow lake and swampy ground, broken by dark patches of reeds and little bushy islands, while on the left a miserable mud village overlooked the water. The sun had barely cleared away the thick, heavy mist, which was still slowly rising here and there, and the jheel birds were wading majestically in search of their breakfast of small fish, and uttering harsh, discordant cries.

To my astonishment, Caulfield seemed a changed man. He was in excellent spirits, his eyes were bright, and the sullen frown had gone from his forehead.

'Isn't it a lovely spot?' he said, laughing and rubbing his

hands. 'Beyond that village the snipe ought to rise in thousands from the rice fields. We shan't be able to shoot it all in three days, worse luck, but we'll keep it dark, and come again. Let's have breakfast. I don't want to lose any time.'

Half an hour later we started, our guns over our shoulders, and a couple of servants behind us carrying the luncheon and cartridge bags. My spirits rose with Caulfield's, for I felt we had the certainty of an excellent day's sport before us.

But the birds were unaccountably wild and few and far between, and luck seemed dead against us. 'Some brutes' had evidently been there before us and harried the birds, was Caulfield's opinion, delivered with disappointed rage, and after tramping and wading all day, we returned, weary and crestfallen, with only a few couple of snipe and half a dozen teal between us. Caulfield was so angry he could hardly eat any dinner, and afterwards sat cursing his luck and the culprits who had forestalled us, till we could neither of us keep awake any longer.

The next morning we took a different route from the previous day, but with no better result. On and on, and round and round we tramped, with only an occasional shot here and there, and at last, long after midday, we sat wearily down to eat our luncheon. I was ravenously hungry, and greedily devoured my share of the provisions, but Caulfield hardly touched a mouthful, and only sat moodily examining his gun, and taking long pulls from his whisky flask. We were seated on the roots of a large tamarind tree, close to the village, and the place had a dreary, depressing appearance. The yellow mud walls were ruined and crumbling, and the inhabitants seemed scanty and poverty-stricken. Two ragged old women were squatting a short distance off, watching us with dim, apathetic eyes, and a few naked children were playing near them, while some bigger boys were driving two or three lean buffaloes towards the water.

Presently another figure came in sight—a fakir, or mendicant priest, as was evident by the tawny masses of wool woven amongst his own black locks and hanging in ropes below his shoulders, the ashes smeared over the almost naked body, and the hollow gourd for alms which he held in his hand. The man's face was long and thin, and his pointed teeth glistened in the sunlight as he demanded money in a dismal monotone. Caulfield flung a pebble at him and told him roughly to be off, with the result that the man slowly disappeared behind a clump of tall, feathery grass.

'Did you notice that brute's face?' said Caulfield as we rose to start again. 'He must have been a pariah dog in a former existence. He was exactly like one!'

'Or a jackal perhaps,' I answered carelessly. 'He looked more like a wild beast.'

Then we walked on, skirting the village and plunging into the damp, soft rice fields. We put up a wisp of snipe, which we followed till we had shot them nearly all, and then, to our joy, we heard a rush of wings overhead, and a lot of duck went down into the corner of a jheel in front of us.

'We've got 'em!' said Caulfield, and we hurried on till we were almost within shot of the birds, and could hear them calling to each other in their fancied security. But suddenly they rose again in wild confusion, and with loud cries of alarm were out of range in a second. Caulfield swore, and so did I, and our rage was increased tenfold when the disturber of the birds appeared in sight, and proved to be the fakir who had paid us a visit at luncheon-time. Caulfield shook his fist at the man and abused him freely in Hindustani but without moving a muscle of his dog-like face the fakir passed us and continued on his way.

Words could not describe Caulfield's vexation.

'They were pin-tail, all of them,' he said, 'and the first decent chance we've had since we came out. To think of that beastly fakir spoiling the whole show, and I don't suppose he had the least idea what he had done.'

'Probably not,' I replied, 'unless there was some spite in it because you threw a stone at him that time.'

'Well, come along,' said Caulfield, with resignation, 'we must make haste as it will be dark soon, and I want to try a place over by those palms before we knock off. We may as well let the servants go back as they've had a hard day. Have you got some cartridges in your pocket?'

'Yes, plenty,' I answered, and after despatching the two men back to the camp with what little game we had got, we walked on in silence.

The sun was sinking in a red ball and the air was heavy with damp, as the white mist stole slowly over the still, cold jheels. Far overhead came the first faint cackle of the wild geese returning home for the night, and presently as we approached the clump of palms we saw more water glistening between the rough stems, and on it, to our delight, a multitude of duck and teal.

But the next moment there was a whir-r-r of wings like the rumble of thunder, and a dense mass of birds flew straight into the air and wheeled bodily away, while the sharp, cold atmosphere resounded with their startled cries. Caulfield said nothing, but he set his jaw and walked rapidly forward, while I followed. We skirted the group of palms, and on the other side we came upon our friend the fakir, who had again succeeded in spoiling our sport. The long, lanky figure was drawn to its full height, the white eyeballs and jagged teeth caught the red glint of the setting sun, and he waved his hand triumphantly in the direction of the vanishing cloud of birds.

Then there came the loud report of a gun, and the next thing I saw was a quivering body on the ground, and wild eyes staring open in the agony of death. Caulfield had shot the fakir, and now he stood looking down at what he had done, while I knelt beside the body and tried hopelessly to persuade myself that life was not extinct. When I got up we gazed at each other for a moment in silence.

'What are we to do?' I asked presently.

'Well, you know what it means,' Caulfield said in a queer, hard voice. 'Killing a native is no joke in these days, and I should come out of it pretty badly.'

I glanced at the body in horror. The face was rigid, and seemed more beast-like than ever. I looked at Caulfield again before I spoke, hesitatingly.

'Of course the whole thing was unpremeditated—an accident.'

'No, it wasn't,' he said defiantly, 'I meant to shoot the brute, and it served him right. And you can't say anything else if it comes out. But I don't see why anyone should know about it but ourselves.'

'It's nasty business,' I said, my heart sinking at the suggestion of concealment.

'It will be nastier still if we don't keep it dark, and you won't like having to give me away, you know. Either we must bury the thing here and say nothing about it, or else we must take it back to the station and stand the devil's own fuss. Probably I shall be kicked out of the service.'

'Of course I'll stand by you,' I said with an effort, 'but we can't do anything this minute. We'd better hide it in that long grass and come back after dinner. We must have something to dig with.'

Caulfield agreed sullenly, and between us we pushed the body in amongst the thick, coarse grass, which completely concealed it, and then made our way back to the camp. We ordered dinner and pretended to eat it, after which we sat for half an hour smoking, until the plates were cleared away and the servants had left the tent. Then I put my hunting-knife into my pocket, and Caulfield picked up a kitchen chopper that his bearer had left lying on the floor, after hammering a stiff joint of a camp chair, and we quitted the tent casually as though intending to have a stroll in the moonlight, which was almost as bright as day. We walked slowly at first, gradually increasing our pace as we left the camp behind us, and Caulfield never spoke a word until we came close to the tall grass that hid the fakir's body. Then he suddenly clutched my arm.

'God in heaven!' he whispered, pointing ahead, 'What is that?'

I saw the grass moving, and heard a scraping sound that made my heart stand still. We moved forward in desperation and parted the grass with our hands. A large jackal was lying on the fakir's body, grinning and snarling at being disturbed over his hideous meal.

'Drive it away,' said Caulfield, hoarsely. But the brute refused to move, and as it lay there showing its teeth, its face reminded me horribly of the wretched man dead beneath its feet. I turned sick and faint, so Caulfield shouted and shook the grass and threw clods of soil at the animal, which rose at last and slunk slowly away. It was an unusually large jackal, more like a wolf, and had lost one of its ears. The coat was rough, and mangy and thickly sprinkled with grey.

For more than an hour we worked desperately with the chopper and hunting-knife, being greatly aided in our task by a rift in the ground where the soil had been softened by water running from the jheel, and finally we stood up with the sweat pouring from our faces, and stamped down the earth which now covered all traces of Caulfield's crime. We had filled the grave with some large stones that were lying about (remnants of some ancient temple, long ago deserted and forgotten), thus feeling secure that it could not easily be disturbed by animals.

The next morning we returned to the station, and Caulfield shut himself up more than ever. He entirely dropped his shooting, which before had been his one pleasure, and the only person he ever spoke to, unofficially, was myself.

The end of April came with its plague of insects and scorching winds. The hours grew long and weary with the heat, and dust storms howled and swirled over the station, bringing perhaps a few tantalizing drops of rain, of more often leaving the air thick with a copper-coloured haze.

One night when it was too hot to sleep, Caulfield suddenly appeared in my verandah and asked me to let him stay the night in my bungalow.

'I know I'm an ass,' he said in awkward apology, 'but I can't stay by myself. I get all sorts of beastly ideas.'

I asked no questions, but gave him a cheroot and tried to cheer him up, telling him scraps of gossip, and encouraging him to talk, when a sound outside made us both start. It proved to be only the weird, plaintive cry of a jackal, but Caulfield sprang to his feet, shaking all over.

'There it is again!' he exclaimed. 'It has followed me over here. Listen!' turning his haggard, sleepless eyes on me. 'Every night that brute comes and howls round my house, and I tell you, on my oath, it's the same jackal we saw eating the poor devil I shot.'

'Nonsense, my dear chap,' I said, pushing him back into the chair, 'you must have got fever. Jackals come and howl round my house all night. That's nothing.'

'Look here,' said Caulfield, very calmly, 'I have no more fever than you have, and if you imagine I am delirious you are mistaken.' He lowered his voice. 'I looked out one night and saw the brute. It had only one ear!'

In spite of my own common sense and the certainty that Caulfield was not himself, my blood ran cold, and after I had succeeded in quieting him and he had dropped off to sleep on the couch, I sat in my long chair for hours, going over in my mind every detail of that horrible night in the jungle.

Several times after this Caulfield came to me and repeated the same tale. He swore he was being haunted by the jackal we had driven away from the fakir's body, and finally took it into his head that the spirit of the murdered man had entered the animal and was bent on obtaining vengeance.

Then he suddenly ceased coming over to me, and when I went to see him he would hardly speak, and only seemed anxious to get rid of me. I urged him to take leave or see a doctor, but he angrily refused to do either, and said he wished I would keep away from him altogether. So I left him alone for a couple of days, but on the third evening my conscience pricked me for having neglected him, and I was preparing to go over to his bungalow, when his bearer rushed in with a face of terror and besought me to come without delay. He said he feared his master was dying, and he had already sent for the doctor. The latter arrived in Caulfield's verandah simultaneously with myself, and together we entered the sick man's room. Caulfield was lying unconscious on his bed.

'He had a sort of fit, sahib,' said the frightened bearer, and proceeded to explain how his master had behaved.

The doctor bent over the bed.

'Do you happen to know if he had been bitten by a dog lately?' he asked, looking up at me.

'Not to my knowledge,' I answered, while the faint wail of a jackal out across the plain struck a chill to my heart.

For twenty-four hours we stayed with Caulfield, watching the terrible struggles we were powerless to relieve, and which lasted till the end came. He was never able to speak after the first paroxysm, which had occurred before we arrived, so we could not learn from him whether he had been bitten or not, neither could the doctor discover any scar on his body which might have been made by the teeth of an animal. Yet there was no shadow of doubt that Caulfield's death was due to hydrophobia.

As we stood in the next room when all was over, drinking the dead man's whisky and soda, which we badly needed, we questioned the bearer closely, but he could tell us little or nothing. His master, he said, did not keep dogs, nor had the bearer ever heard of his having been bitten by one; but there had been a mad jackal about the place nearly three weeks ago which his master had tried to shoot but failed.

'It couldn't have been that,' said the doctor, 'he would have come to me if he had been bitten by a jackal.'

'No,' I answered mechanically, 'it could not have been that.' And I went into the bedroom to take a last look at poor Caulfield's thin, white face with its ghastly, hunted expression, for there was now nothing more that I could do for him.

Then I picked up a lantern and stepped out into the dark verandah, intending to go home. As I did so, something came silently round the corner of the house and stood in my path. I raised my lantern and caught a glimpse of a mass of grey fur, two fiery yellow eyes, and bared, glistening teeth. It was only a stray jackal, and I struck at it with my stick, but instead of running away it slipped past me and entered Caulfield's room. The light fell on the animal's head, and I saw that it had only one ear.

In a frenzy I rushed back into the house calling for the doctor and servants.

'I saw a jackal come in here,' I said, searching round the bedroom, 'hunt it out at once.'

Every nook and corner was examined, but no jackal was found.

'Go home to bed, my boy, and keep quiet till I come and see you in the morning,' said the doctor, looking at me keenly. 'This business has shaken your nerves, and your imagination is beginning to play you tricks. Goodnight.'

'Goodnight,' I answered, and went slowly back to my bungalow, trying to persuade myself that he was right.

DOWN ELEPHANT STREET

K.M. Eady

Maclaren was having his first experience of jungle marching, and, although Punch, when a little fellow, had seen something of that sort of work, it had never been through such tangle as this.

The forest trees, densely matted overhead, and each, in its turn, overgrown with thick masses of orchids and other creepers, so that the monkeys could race from tree-top to tree-top without a break, shut out the light of the sun and the cooling breezes from the human wayfarers below, while beneath, in the damp, stifling, oppressive heat, there seemed to be every kind of shrub and creeper that Nature could produce, capable of growing a thorn or sharp, sword-edged leaf to tear and wound the unwary passer-by.

The two lads made very slow progress, but that was only to be expected; the worst feature of the case was that it was by no means sure. They had no compass, they could not see the sun, and, in the soft, dim twilight of the forest, all paths—or rather, absence of paths—looked the same. After some time a vague fear began to oppress Punch that they might not be keeping their course correctly, and he was considerably upset to find that Maclaren shared his fears, but their dismay was complete when, one evening, they came back to their last night's resting-place, and discovered that the day's march had been in a circle.

Both lads flung themselves down on the ground, and looked at each other in speechless dread. At length Punch spoke, 'A whole day lost!' he groaned, 'and perhaps that fellow Ismail close behind us!'

'And, this may not be the first day that we've done the same thing,' Maclaren added, still more dejectedly.

'And, it may not be the last,' Punch suggested with a gasp.

'Oh! hang it, old fellow, now we know, we shall be able to prevent it,' Maclaren interposed hastily. 'We must fix on some big tree ahead, and keep straight on, and—'

'But that's what we have been trying to do all the time! Don't you see, old fellow, we can only see the trees a few yards ahead of us, and, when we reach one mark, we can't be sure that the next one is really straight ahead.'

This was, unfortunately, only too true, as many a traveller had discovered before them. They discussed the matter at length before settling down to rest, but could find no real solution to their difficulty. They resolved to be more careful, to mark each distinct clump of trees in their minds as they passed, and, for the rest, to push on steadily and hope for the best, but it was with considerable misgiving that they started once more.

They dared not stray into the jungle in pursuit of game, but a continuous vegetable diet, and that a very sparing one, became exceedingly monotonous. When a herd crossed their path, or a single animal started up from under their feet, they were able now and again to spear a little wild pig, and once managed to secure one of the pretty little hogdeer which Maclaren had never seen before; but they always felt that the lighting of a fire, even in this dense forest, was dangerous work, and might bring their human enemies on them, while the scent of blood might attract other, and equally undesirable foes. Indeed, one night, when a portion of cooked hog's meat had been put aside, well wrapped in leaves, for the morrow, it was found to have been carried away by some noiseless visitor, and it was only by the tracks on the soft ground that the lads could gather how great a risk they had run of being mauled or killed.

But they were fated to pass through a far worse danger than this. One day, they had been making their way as usual through dense jungle, from time to time obliged to cut a path through the thicket of underwood and trailing creepers, and seeing only a few yards ahead into the dim recesses of the dark, silent forest. Suddenly Punch, who was leading, stopped short, and peered through the bushes at some unusual sight.

'What is it?' Maclaren whispered, coming to his side.

'A clearing. Look—straight ahead,' and he pointed through the trees to where unmistakably a clearing had been made, not only in the underwood, but among the lesser trees.

'Is it those dwarf fellows again, or—or Malays' and Maclarerfs whisper betrayed his anxiety.

'I don't know; neither, I think. 'We have heard no axes, and, see——that tree has been uprooted, not cut down! Come on very carefully, and we'll spy out the land.'

With extreme caution they stole on, skirting the open space for fear of ambushed foes, but seeking for some spot where, themselves sheltered, they could view the clearing more closely. At length one was found, and then, leaning forward over the branch of a tree on its outskirts, the opening could be clearly observed.

It covered a considerable space, but appeared to have been

roughly made, for its boundaries were uneven, and the trees and shrubs had been selected from all spots and of all kinds, and had been thrown down, singly or in heaps, in the wildest confusion. Some were strong young saplings, torn up bodily by the roots, tree ferns were pushed down, and pressed and broken into a heap of crushed bushes, and all the lower and smaller growth, had been trodden down into the miry ground below, which again was full of the marks of huge footsteps. Beyond, on the one side, a broad lane of broken and down-trodden shrubs showed whence the intruders had come, while another broad lane, nearly opposite, marked the spot of their exit, and, throughout both, lopped branches and torn down creepers, half-eaten and then thrown away, told their own tale of destruction, apparently quite as much for amusement as for food.

Punch laughed aloud, and sprang out fearlessly into the opening. 'Elephants,' he said reassuringly, as his companion followed him more cautiously. 'They've gone on, hours ago, after making hay very considerably here. There must have been a lot of them,' he added, as he tried to distinguish the footmarks.

'Elephants!' Maclaren repeated. 'Do you mean to say that they can make a clearing like this? Why, it would take a small army of woodmen to cut down all those trees.'

'No doubt, but it's child's play to a hungry elephant to haul up a tree, for the sake of a few leaves on its crown, perhaps. They're queer beasts. They seem to delight in smashing things about just for the fun of it. Look, some of those trees haven't been touched for food.'

'I wish we had been earlier and could have seen them,' Maclaren said eagerly. 'A herd of wild elephants very much at home in the jungle would have been a sight worth seeing.'

'Yes, *if* we had a couple of good rifles and were dead shots,'

Punch replied with unusual gravity. 'As it is, the less we see of them the better. If we came across them and scared them, especially if there were any old cow elephants with young calves among them, they would charge like a shot, and'—he looked round expressively at the mass of destruction at their feet—'you can guess pretty well how we should come out of the business.'

'H'm!' Maclaren's sporting aspirations died away suddenly. 'Yes, they would make hay, as you call it, of us very easily. So, I suppose we mustn't use that road over there which they have so kindly made for us.'

'I don't know about that,' Punch replied doubtfully. 'They passed some time ago, and may have gone miles ahead by this time; on the other hand, they may be feeding or sleeping close by. They sleep a good deal in the daytime, I believe. Anyway, I think we may safely use their road for a bit, but we must keep a sharp look out, hold our tongues, tread softly, and, if we see or hear them, make for a big tree, and stay up in it until they move on. It wouldn't waste more time than cutting our way through this hateful jungle.'

'Don't abuse the jungle,' Maclaren laughed. 'It helped us out of Ismail's clutches.'

'We aren't out of the wood yet, literally or otherwise,' Punch replied, not very consolingly. 'Come on, old fellow, here goes for a trot down Elephant Street!'

It was certainly a relief to find a broad and comparatively smooth path prepared for them, and for some two miles or more it led onwards in a fairly straight course, and, so far as the lads could judge, in the direction of Disting. So far, so good, but it was with considerable trepidation that both kept their eyes fixed steadily forward, looking ahead eagerly for new dangers. At length they reached a slight incline, where the path led straight up to its summit, but, of course beyond that point, further views, except of the thick wall of tree-tops below, were shut out by the hill itself. Very cautiously the lads stole up, endeavouring, with care learnt by experience, to avoid treading on dry twigs, or striking the boot against trunks or roots of trees.

They reached the top and looked down on a very curious sight. Below them lay a small, hollow, cup-shaped space, cleared, like the former opening, of all shrubs and smaller trees, and, among the litter of broken wood and disordered foliage, either asleep or lazily chewing the green food at their sides, lay a number of elephants. Several were large old tuskers, but, to Punch's dismay, he discerned among them two or three calves, and he knew that the mothers, always more vigilant than the males, would now be unusually watchful and fierce. If they should discover the presence of human beings, a charge was inevitable, and old stories, told him years before by European and native hunters, warned him of the extreme danger to themselves, practically unarmed as they were, of such a course.

He touched Maclaren on the shoulder, pointed to two big trees near the path, and sufficiently stout to withstand the charge of the strongest elephant, and made hurriedly but silently for one.

Maclaren followed him with equal haste and caution, but it was almost too late. Despite all their care, some sound must have been overheard, or perhaps the wind carried the scent of man—deadliest and most dreaded foe of all wild beasts—to some wakeful member of the slumbering herd, for, with a shrill scream of alarm, a huge, cow-elephant scrambled to her feet. The others followed her example, and for a moment all was confusion, before the herd closed up together, and stood, perfectly still, as though puzzling out the cause of the alarm. Then the first to move, forcing her way through the herd, threw up her trunk, and waved it in the air to catch the direction of the scent, then it was as rapidly drawn down, curled up, and she started to charge.

She came up the hill with almost incredible rapidity, and Maclaren, although most of his energies were devoted to the task of clambering up the tree trunk, regardless of prickly creepers and torn hands, face, and clothing, was yet able to observe, with considerable astonishment, the wonderful grace and dignity of the animal's movements. His former experience of elephants had been of domesticated beasts, performing various tasks in such a way as to exhibit them at their worst, their huge size and strength only increasing the awkwardness of their movements. But now, in her native forests, surrounded by giant vegetation, and moving in her silent wrath with great easy strides, very swiftly, but smoothly and regularly, there was something grand and majestic in this charge.

However, Maclaren had little time to notice all this, and to Punch, who had often before been an interested spectator at an elephant hunt, if not an actual hunter, there was nothing novel in the business, except the fact that the usual quarry was hunting the men, instead of the men hunting the elephant. He was already well up his tree, out of the reach of both tusks and trunk, and now turned anxiously to see how Maclaren was faring. But the sailor had not been equally fortunate. While he was still only some eight or ten feet from the ground the elephant sighted him, and, with another shrill snort of fury, prepared to charge.

Maclaren had not been at sea for six years for nothing. He caught at the branches above him with frantic haste, and hauled himself up with all possible speed, but even then he could not have got out of the way in time if Punch had not created a diversion in his favour.

The boy knew that it would be impossible to do serious

damage to the huge brute with the poor weapon, a stout, iron—tipped, bamboo spear, which was all that he possessed, but he also knew how easily the anger of the elephant could be diverted for the time being, and he launched the spear with all his force against her great flapping ear. It sped truly and struck home, and the animal screamed once more with rage and pain, turned round, and charged straight at Punch's tree.

But here even her great strength could do little damage, for the great stem, although it rocked and creaked at each of her frantic charges, could have withstood greater force than she could bring to bear against it, and the boy was out of her reach, sitting astride a branch well above her head. She soon realized this and returned to Maclaren, but he had taken advantage of the few moments' respite to climb as high as Punch himself, and, beyond a few splinters, and much swaying and groaning, his tree was none the worse for her attack.

The remainder of the herd had galloped away into the jungle, but from time to time came an appealing cry from her deserted calf, and at length the old elephant seemed weary of her fruitless attack. She looked from the one tree to the other, eyeing the two lads keenly with her little bright eyes, then, with one more angry scream, she dashed off to join her companions.

The danger was over for the present, but she might return, and the two young fellows thought it wise to remain for a considerable time in their leafy shelter. Then, at length, they ventured to descend and resume their march, but this time they preferred to take their own path, even at the risk of travelling once more in a circle.

PANTHER'S MOON

Ruskin Bond

I

In the entire village, he was the first to get up. Even the dog, a big hill mastiff called Sheroo, was asleep in a corner of the dark room, curled up near the cold embers of the previous night's fire. Bisnu's tousled head emerged from his blanket. He rubbed the sleep from his eyes and sat up on his haunches. Then, gathering his wits, he crawled in the direction of the loud ticking that came from the battered little clock which occupied the second most honoured place in a niche in the wall. The most honoured place belonged to a picture of Ganesha, the god of learning, who had an elephant's head and a fat boy's body.

Bringing his face close to the clock, Bisnu could just make out the hands. It was five o'clock. He had half an hour in which to get ready and leave.

He got up, in vest and underpants, and moved quietly towards the door. The soft tread of his bare feet woke Sheroo, and the big black dog rose silently and padded behind the boy. The door opened and closed, and then the boy and the dog were outside in the early dawn. The month was June, and the nights were warm, even in the Himalayan valleys; but there was fresh dew on the grass. Bisnu felt the dew beneath his feet. He took a deep breath and began walking down to the stream.

The sound of the stream filled the small valley. At that early hour of the morning, it was the only sound; but Bisnu was hardly conscious of it. It was a sound he lived with and took for granted. It was only when he had crossed the hill, on his way to the town—and the sound of the stream grew distant—that he really began to notice it. And it was only when the stream was too far away to be heard that he really missed its sound.

He slipped out of his underclothes, gazed for a few moments at the goose pimples rising on his flesh, and then dashed into the shallow stream. As he went further in, the cold mountain water reached his loins and navel, and he gasped with shock and pleasure. He drifted slowly with the current, swam across to a small inlet which formed a fairly deep pool, and plunged into the water. Sheroo hated cold water at this early hour. Had the sun been up, he would not have hesitated to join Bisnu. Now he contented himself with sitting on a smooth rock and gazing placidly at the slim brown boy splashing about in the clear water, in the widening light of dawn.

Bisnu did not stay long in the water. There wasn't time. When he returned to the house, he found his mother up, making tea and chapattis. His sister, Puja, was still asleep. She was a little older than Bisnu, a pretty girl with large black eyes, good teeth and strong arms and legs. During the day, she helped her mother in the house and in the fields. She did not go to the school with Bisnu. But when he came home in the evenings, he would try teaching her some of the things he had learnt. Their father was dead. Bisnu, at twelve, considered himself the head of the family.

He ate two chapattis, after spreading butter-oil on them. He drank a glass of hot sweet tea. His mother gave two thick chapattis to Sheroo, and the dog wolfed them down in a few minutes. Then she wrapped two chapattis and a gourd curry in some big green leaves, and handed these to Bisnu. This was his lunch packet. His mother and Puja would take their meal afterwards.

When Bisnu was dressed, he stood with folded hands before the picture of Ganesha. Ganesha is the god who blesses all beginnings. The author who begins to write a new book, the banker who opens a new ledger, the traveller who starts on a journey, all invoke the kindly help of Ganesha. And as Bisnu made a journey every day, he never left without the goodwill of the elephant-headed god.

How, one might ask, did Ganesha get his elephant's head?

When born, he was a beautiful child. Parvati, his mother, was so proud of him that she went about showing him to everyone. Unfortunately she made the mistake of showing the child to that envious planet, Saturn, who promptly burnt off poor Ganesha's head. Parvati in despair went to Brahma, the Creator, for a new head for her son. He had no head to give her, but advised her to search for some man or animal caught in a sinful or wrong act. Parvati wandered about until she came upon an elephant sleeping with its head the wrong way, that is, to the south. She promptly removed the elephant's head and planted it on Ganesha's shoulders, where it took root.

Bisnu knew this story. He had heard it from his mother.

Wearing a white shirt and black shorts, and a pair of worn white keds, he was ready for his long walk to school, five miles up the mountain.

His sister woke up just as he was about to leave. She pushed the hair away from her face and gave Bisnu one of her rare smiles.

'I hope you have not forgotten,' she said.

'Forgotten?' said Bisnu, pretending innocence. 'Is there anything I am supposed to remember?'

'Don't tease me. You promised to buy me a pair of bangles, remember? I hope you won't spend the money on sweets, as you did last time.'

'Oh, yes, your bangles,' said Bisnu. 'Girls have nothing better to do than waste money on trinkets. Now, don't lose your temper! I'll get them for you. Red and gold are the colours you want?'

'Yes, brother,' said Puja gently, pleased that Bisnu had remembered the colours. 'And for your dinner tonight we'll make you something special. Won't we, Mother?'

'Yes. But hurry up and dress. There is some ploughing to be done today. The rains will soon be here, if the gods are kind.'

'The monsoon will be late this year,' said Bisnu. 'Mr Nautiyal, our teacher, told us so. He said it had nothing to do with the gods.'

'Be off, you are getting late,' said Puja, before Bisnu could begin an argument with his mother. She was diligently winding the old clock. It was quite light in the room. The sun would be up any minute.

Bisnu shouldered his school bag, kissed his mother, pinched his sister's cheeks and left the house. He started climbing the steep path up the mountainside. Sheroo bounded ahead; for he, too, always went with Bisnu to school.

Five miles to school. Every day, except Sunday, Bisnu walked five miles to school; and in the evening, he walked home again.

There was no school in his own small village of Manjari, for the village consisted of only five families. The nearest school was at Kemptee, a small township on the bus route through the district of Garhwal. A number of boys walked to school, from distances of two or three miles; their villages were not quite as remote as Manjari. But Bisnu's village lay right at the bottom of the mountain, a drop of over 2,000 feet from Kemptee. There was no proper road between the village and the town.

In Kemptee there was a school, a small mission hospital, a post office and several shops. In Manjari village there were none of these amenities. If you were sick, you stayed at home until you got well; if you were very sick, you walked or were carried to the hospital, up the five-mile path. If you wanted to buy something, you went without it; but if you wanted it very badly, you could walk the five miles to Kemptee.

Manjari was known as the Five-Mile Village.

Twice a week, if there were any letters, a postman came to the village. Bisnu usually passed the postman on his way to and from school.

There were other boys in Manjari village, but Bisnu was the only one who went to school. His mother would not have fussed if he had stayed at home and worked in the fields. That was what the other boys did; all except lazy Chittru, who preferred fishing in the stream or helping himself to the fruit off other people's trees. But Bisnu went to school. He went because he wanted to. No one could force him to go; and no one could stop him from going. He had set his heart on receiving a good schooling. He wanted to read and write as well as anyone in the big world, the world that seemed to begin only where the mountains ended. He felt cut off from the world in his small valley. He would rather live at the top of a mountain than at the bottom of one. That was why he liked climbing to Kemptee, it took him to the top of the mountain; and from its ridge he could look down on his own valley to the north, and on the wide endless plains stretching towards the south.

The plainsman looks to the hills for the needs of his spirit but the hill man looks to the plains for a living.

Leaving the village and the fields below him, Bisnu climbed steadily up the bare hillside, now dry and brown. By the time the sun was up, he had entered the welcome shade of an oak and rhododendron forest. Sheroo went bounding ahead, chasing squirrels and barking at langoors.

A colony of langoors lived in the oak forest. They fed on oak leaves, acorns and other green things, and usually remained in the trees, coming down to the ground only to play or bask in the sun. They were beautiful, supple-limbed animals, with black faces and silver-grey coats and long, sensitive tails. They leapt from tree to tree with great agility. The young ones wrestled on the grass like boys.

A dignified community, the langoors did not have the cheekiness or dishonest habits of the red monkeys of the plains; they did not approach dogs or humans. But they had grown used to Bisnu's comings and goings, and did not fear him. Some of the older ones would watch him quietly, a little puzzled. They did not go near the town, because the Kemptee boys threw stones at them. And anyway, the oak forest gave them all the food they required.

Emerging from the trees, Bisnu crossed a small brook. Here he stopped to drink the fresh clean water of a spring. The brook tumbled down the mountain and joined the river a little below Bisnu's village. Coming from another direction was a second path, and at the junction of the two paths Sarru was waiting for him.

Sarru came from a small village about three miles from Bisnu's and closer to the town. He had two large milk cans slung over his shoulders. Every morning he carried this milk to town, selling one can to the school and the other to Mrs Taylor, the lady doctor at the small mission hospital. He was a little older than Bisnu but not as well-built.

They hailed each other, and Sarru fell into step beside Bisnu. They often met at this spot, keeping each other company for the remaining two miles to Kemptee.

'There was a panther in our village last night,' said Sarru.

This information interested but did not excite Bisnu. Panthers were common enough in the hills and did not usually present a problem except during the winter months, when their natural prey was scarce. Then, occasionally, a panther would take to haunting the outskirts of a village, seizing a careless dog or a stray goat.

'Did you lose any animals?' asked Bisnu.

'No. It tried to get into the cowshed but the dogs set up an alarm. We drove it off.'

'It must be the same one which came around last winter. We lost a calf and two dogs in our village.'

'Wasn't that the one the shikaris wounded? I hope it hasn't become a cattle lifter.'

'It could be the same. It has a bullet in its leg. These hunters are the people who cause all the trouble. They think it's easy to shoot a panther. It would be better if they missed altogether, but they usually wound it.'

'And then the panther's too slow to catch the barking deer, and starts on our own animals.'

'We're lucky it didn't become a man-eater. Do you

remember the man-eater six years ago? I was very small then. My father told me all about it. Ten people were killed in our valley alone. What happened to it?'

'I don't know. Some say it poisoned itself when it ate the headman of another village.'

Bisnu laughed. 'No one liked that old villain. He must have been a man-eater himself in some previous existence!' They linked arms and scrambled up the stony path. Sheroo began barking and ran ahead. Someone was coming down the path.

It was Mela Ram, the postman.

II

'Any letters for us?' asked Bisnu and Sarru together.

They never received any letters but that did not stop them from asking. It was one way of finding out who had received letters.

'You're welcome to all of them,' said Mela Ram, 'if you'll carry my bag for me.'

'Not today,' said Sarru. 'We're busy today. Is there a letter from Corporal Ghanshyam for his family?'

'Yes, there is a postcard for his people. He is posted on the Ladakh border now and finds it very cold there.'

Postcards, unlike sealed letters, were considered public property and were read by everyone. The senders knew that too, and so Corporal Ghanshyam Singh was careful to mention that he expected a promotion very soon. He wanted everyone in his village to know it.

Mela Ram, complaining of sore feet, continued on his way, and the boys carried on up the path. It was eight o'clock when they reached Kemptee. Dr Taylor's outpatients were just beginning to trickle in at the hospital gate. The doctor was trying to prop up a rose creeper which had blown down during the night. She liked attending to her plants in the mornings, before starting on her patients. She found this helped her in her work. There was a lot in common between ailing plants and ailing people.

Dr Taylor was fifty, white-haired but fresh in the face and full of vitality. She had been in India for twenty years, and ten of these had been spent working in the hill regions.

She saw Bisnu coming down the road. She knew about the boy and his long walk to school and admired him for his keenness and sense of purpose. She wished there were more like him.

Bisnu greeted her shyly. Sheroo barked and put his paws up on the gate.

'Yes, there's a bone for you,' said Dr Taylor. She often put aside bones for the big black dog, for she knew that Bisnu's people could not afford to give the dog a regular diet of meat—though he did well enough on milk and chapattis.

She threw the bone over the gate and Sheroo caught it before it fell. The school bell began ringing and Bisnu broke into a run. Sheroo loped along behind the boy.

When Bisnu entered the school gate, Sheroo sat down on the grass of the compound. He would remain there until the lunchbreak. He knew of various ways of amusing himself during school hours and had friends among the bazaar dogs. But just then he didn't want company. He had his bone to get on with.

Mr Nautiyal, Bisnu's teacher, was in a bad mood. He was a keen rose grower and only that morning, on getting up and looking out of his bedroom window, he had been horrified to see a herd of goats in his garden. He had chased them down the road with a stick but the damage had already been done.

His prize roses had all been consumed.

Mr Nautiyal had been so upset that he had gone without his breakfast. He had also cut himself whilst shaving. Thus, his mood had gone from bad to worse. Several times during the day, he brought down his ruler on the knuckles of any boy who irritated him. Bisnu was one of his best pupils. But even Bisnu irritated him by asking too many questions about a new sum which Mr Nautiyal didn't feel like explaining.

That was the kind of day it was for Mr Nautiyal. Most schoolteachers know similar days.

'Poor Mr Nautiyal,' thought Bisnu. 'I wonder why he's so upset. It must be because of his pay. He doesn't get much money. But he's a good teacher. I hope he doesn't take another job.'

But after Mr Nautiyal had eaten his lunch, his mood improved (as it always did after a meal), and the rest of the day passed serenely. Armed with a bundle of homework, Bisnu came out from the school compound at four o'clock, and was immediately joined by Sheroo. He proceeded down the road in the company of several of his classfellows. But he did not linger long in the bazaar. There were five miles to walk, and he did not like to get home too late. Usually, he reached his house just as it was beginning to get dark. Sarru had gone home long ago, and Bisnu had to make the return journey on his own. It was a good opportunity to memorize the words of an English poem he had been asked to learn.

Bisnu had reached the little brook when he remembered the bangles he had promised to buy for his sister.

'Oh, I've forgotten them again,' he said aloud. 'Now I'll catch it—and she's probably made something special for my dinner!'

Sheroo, to whom these words were addressed, paid no attention but bounded off into the oak forest. Bisnu looked around for the monkeys but they were nowhere to be seen.

'Strange,' he thought, 'I wonder why they have disappeared.' He was startled by a sudden sharp cry, followed by a fierce yelp. He knew at once that Sheroo was in trouble. The noise came from the bushes down the khud, into which the dog had rushed but a few seconds previously.

Bisnu jumped off the path and ran down the slope towards the bushes. There was no dog and not a sound. He whistled and called, but there was no response. Then he saw something lying on the dry grass. He picked it up. It was a portion of a dog's collar, stained with blood. It was Sheroo's collar and Sheroo's blood.

Bisnu did not search further. He knew, without a doubt, that Sheroo had been seized by a panther. No other animal could have attacked so silently and swiftly and carried off a big dog without a struggle. Sheroo was dead—must have been dead within seconds of being caught and flung into the air. Bisnu knew the danger that lay in wait for him if he followed the blood trail through the trees. The panther would attack anyone who interfered with its meal. With tears starting in his eyes, Bisnu carried on down the path to the village. His fingers still clutched the little bit of bloodstained collar that was all that was left to him of his dog.

III

Bisnu was not a very sentimental boy, but he sorrowed for his dog who had been his companion on many a hike into the hills and forests. He did not sleep that night, but turned restlessly from side to side moaning softly. After some time he felt Puja's hand on his head. She began stroking his brow. He took her hand in her own and the clasp of her rough, warm familiar hand gave him a feeling of comfort and security.

Next morning, when he went down to the stream to bathe, he missed the presence of his dog. He did not stay long in the water. It wasn't as much fun when there was no Sheroo to watch him.

When Bisnu's mother gave him his food, she told him to be careful and hurry home that evening. A panther, even if it is only a cowardly lifter of sheep or dogs, is not to be trifled with. And this particular panther had shown some daring by seizing the dog even before it was dark.

Still, there was no question of staying away from school. If Bisnu remained at home every time a panther put in an appearance, he might just as well stop going to school altogether.

He set off even earlier than usual and reached the meeting of the paths long before Sarru. He did not wait for his friend, because he did not feel like talking about the loss of his dog. It was not the day for the postman, and so Bisnu reached Kemptee without meeting anyone on the way. He tried creeping past the hospital gate unnoticed, but Dr Taylor saw him and the first thing she said was: 'Where's Sheroo? I've got something for him.'

When Dr Taylor saw the boy's face, she knew at once that something was wrong.

'What is it, Bisnu?' she asked. She looked quickly up and down the road. 'Is it Sheroo?'

He nodded gravely.

'A panther took him,' he said.

'In the village?'

'No, while we were walking home through the forest. I did not see anything—but I heard.'

Dr Taylor knew that there was nothing she could say that would console him, and she tried to conceal the bone which she had brought out for the dog, but Bisnu noticed her hiding it behind her back and the tears welled up in his eyes. He turned away and began running down the road.

His schoolfellows noticed Sheroo's absence and questioned Bisnu. He had to tell them everything. They were full of sympathy, but they were also quite thrilled at what had happened and kept pestering Bisnu for all the details. There was a lot of noise in the classroom, and Mr Nautiyal had to call for order. When he learnt what had happened, he patted Bisnu on the head and told him that he need not attend school for the rest of the day. But Bisnu did not want to go home. After school, he got into a fight with one of the boys, and that helped him forget.

IV

The panther that plunged the village into an atmosphere of gloom and terror may not have been the same panther that took Sheroo. There was no way of knowing, and it would have made no difference, because the panther that came by night and struck at the people of Manjari was that most feared of wild creatures, a man-eater.

Nine-year-old Sanjay, son of Kalam Singh, was the first child to be attacked by the panther.

Kalam Singh's house was the last in the village and nearest the stream. Like the other houses, it was quite small, just a room above and a stable below, with steps leading up from outside the house. He lived there with his wife, two sons (Sanjay was the youngest) and little daughter Basanti who had just turned three.

Sanjay had brought his father's cows home after grazing them on the hillside in the company of other children. He had also brought home an edible wild plant, which his mother cooked into a tasty dish for their evening meal. They had their food at dusk, sitting on the floor of their single room, and soon after settled down for the night. Sanjay curled up in his favourite spot, with his head near the door, where he got a little fresh air. As the nights were warm, the door was usually left a little ajar. Sanjay's mother piled ash on the embers of the fire and the family was soon asleep.

No one heard the stealthy padding of a panther approaching the door, pushing it wider open. But suddenly there were sounds of a frantic struggle, and Sanjay's stifled cries were mixed with the grunts of the panther. Kalam Singh leapt to his feet with a shout. The panther had dragged Sanjay out of the door and was pulling him down the steps, when Kalam Singh started battering at the animal with a large stone. The rest of the family screamed in terror, rousing the entire village. A number of men came to Kalam Singh's assistance, and the panther was driven off. But Sanjay lay unconscious.

Someone brought a lantern and the boy's mother screamed when she saw her small son with his head lying in a pool of blood. It looked as if the side of his head had been eaten off by the panther. But he was still alive, and as Kalam Singh plastered ash on the boy's head to stop the bleeding, he found that though the scalp had been torn off one side of the head, the bare bone was smooth and unbroken.

'He won't live through the night,' said a neighbour. 'We'll have to carry him down to the river in the morning.'

The dead were always cremated on the banks of a small river which flowed past Manjari village.

Suddenly the panther, still prowling about the village, called out in rage and frustration, and the villagers rushed to their homes in panic and barricaded themselves in for the night.

Sanjay's mother sat by the boy for the rest of the night,

weeping and watching. Towards dawn he started to moan and show signs of coming round. At this sign of returning consciousness, Kalam Singh rose determinedly and looked around for his stick.

He told his elder son to remain behind with the mother and daughter, as he was going to take Sanjay to Dr Taylor at the hospital.

'See, he is moaning and in pain,' said Kalam Singh. 'That means he has a chance to live if he can be treated at once.'

With a stout stick in his hand, and Sanjay on his back, Kalam Singh set off on the two miles of hard mountain track to the hospital at Kemptee. His son, a bloodstained cloth around his head, was moaning but still unconscious. When at last Kalam Singh climbed up through the last fields below the hospital, he asked for the doctor and stammered out an account of what had happened.

It was a terrible injury, as Dr Taylor discovered. The bone over almost one-third of the head was bare and the scalp was torn all round. As the father told his story, the doctor cleaned and dressed the wound, and then gave Sanjay a shot of penicillin to prevent sepsis. Later, Kalam Singh carried the boy home again.

V

After this, the panther went away for some time. But the people of Manjari could not be sure of its whereabouts. They kept to their houses after dark and shut their doors. Bisnu had to stop going to school, because there was no one to accompany him and it was dangerous to go alone. This worried him, because his final exam was only a few weeks off and he would be missing important classwork. When he wasn't in the fields, helping with the sowing of rice and maize, he would be sitting in the shade of a chestnut tree, going through his well-thumbed second-hand school books. He had no other reading, except for a copy of the Ramayana and a Hindi translation of *Alice's Adventures in Wonderland*. These were well- preserved, read only in fits and starts, and usually kept locked in his mother's old tin trunk.

Sanjay had nightmares for several nights and woke up screaming. But with the resilience of youth, he quickly recovered. At the end of the week he was able to walk to the hospital, though his father always accompanied him. Even a desperate panther will hesitate to attack a party of two. Sanjay, with his thin little face and huge bandaged head, looked a pathetic figure, but he was getting better and the wound looked healthy.

Bisnu often went to see him, and the two boys spent long hours together near the stream. Sometimes Chittru would join them, and they would try catching fish with a home-made net. They were often successful in taking home one or two mountain trout. Sometimes, Bisnu and Chittru wrestled in the shallow water or on the grassy banks of the stream. Chittru was a chubby boy with a broad chest, strong legs and thighs, and when he used his weight he got Bisnu under him. But Bisnu was hard and wiry and had very strong wrists and fingers. When he had Chittru in a vice, the bigger boy would cry out and give up the struggle. Sanjay could not join in these games.

He had never been a very strong boy and he needed plenty of rest if his wounds were to heal well.

The panther had not been seen for over a week, and the people of Manjari were beginning to hope that it might have moved on over the mountain or further down the valley.

'I think I can start going to school again,' said Bisnu. 'The panther has gone away.'

'Don't be too sure,' said Puja. 'The moon is full these days and perhaps it is only being cautious.'

'Wait a few days,' said their mother. 'It is better to wait. Perhaps you could go the day after tomorrow when Sanjay goes to the hospital with his father. Then you will not be alone.'

And so, two days later, Bisnu went up to Kemptee with Sanjay and Kalam Singh. Sanjay's wound had almost healed over. Little islets of flesh had grown over the bone. Dr Taylor told him that he need come to see her only once a fortnight, instead of every third day.

Bisnu went to his school, and was given a warm welcome by his friends and by Mr Nautiyal.

'You'll have to work hard,' said his teacher. 'You have to catch up with the others. If you like, I can give you some extra time after classes.'

'Thank you, sir, but it will make me late,' said Bisnu. 'I must get home before it is dark, otherwise my mother will worry. I think the panther has gone but nothing is certain.'

'Well, you mustn't take risks. Do your best, Bisnu. Work hard and you'll soon catch up with your lessons.'

Sanjay and Kalam Singh were waiting for him outside the school. Together they took the path down to Manjari, passing the postman on the way. Mela Ram said he had heard that the panther was in another district and that there was nothing to fear. He was on his rounds again.

Nothing happened on the way. The langoors were back in their favourite part of the forest. Bisnu got home just as the kerosene lamp was being lit. Puja met him at the door with a winsome smile.

'Did you get the bangles?' she asked.

But Bisnu had forgotten again.

VI

There had been a thunderstorm and some rain—a short, sharp shower which gave the villagers hope that the monsoon would arrive on time. It brought out the thunder lilies—pink, crocus-like flowers which sprang up on the hillsides immediately after a summer shower.

Bisnu, on his way home from school, was caught in the rain. He knew the shower would not last, so he took shelter in a small cave and, to pass the time, began doing sums, scratching figures in the damp earth with the end of a stick.

When the rain stopped, he came out from the cave and continued down the path. He wasn't in a hurry. The rain had made everything smell fresh and good. The scent from fallen pine needles rose from wet earth. The leaves of the oak trees had been washed clean and a light breeze turned them about, showing their silver undersides. The birds, refreshed and high-spirited, set up a terrific noise. The worst offenders were the yellow-bottomed bulbuls who squabbled and fought in the blackberry bushes. A barbet, high up in the branches of a deodar, set up its querulous, plaintive call. And a flock of bright green parrots came swooping down the hill to settle in a wild plum tree and feast on the unripe fruit. The langoors, too, had been revived by the rain. They leapt friskily from tree to tree greeting Bisnu with little grunts.

He was almost out of the oak forest when he heard a faint bleating. Presently, a little goat came stumbling up the path towards him. The kid was far from home and must have strayed from the rest of the herd. But it was not yet conscious of being lost. It came to Bisnu with a hop, skip and a jump and started nuzzling against his legs like a cat.

'I wonder who you belong to,' mused Bisnu, stroking the little creature. 'You'd better come home with me until someone claims you.'

He didn't have to take the kid in his arms. It was used to humans and followed close at his heels. Now that darkness was coming on, Bisnu walked a little faster.

He had not gone very far when he heard the sawing grunt of a panther.

The sound came from the hill to the right, and Bisnu judged the distance to be anything from a hundred to two hundred yards. He hesitated on the path, wondering what to do. Then he picked the kid up in his arms and hurried on in the direction of home and safety.

The panther called again, much closer now. If it was an ordinary panther, it would go away on finding that the kid was with Bisnu. If it was the man-eater, it would not hesitate to attack the boy, for no man-eater fears a human. There was no time to lose and there did not seem much point in running. Bisnu looked up and down the hillside. The forest was far behind him and there were only a few trees in his vicinity. He chose a spruce.

The branches of the Himalayan spruce are very brittle and snap easily beneath a heavy weight. They were strong enough to support Bisnu's light frame. It was unlikely they would take the weight of a full-grown panther. At least that was what Bisnu hoped.

Holding the kid with one arm, Bisnu gripped a low branch and swung himself up into the tree. He was a good climber. Slowly but confidently he climbed half-way up the tree, until he was about twelve feet above the ground. He couldn't go any higher without risking a fall.

He had barely settled himself in the crook of a branch when the panther came into the open, running into the clearing at a brisk trot. This was no stealthy approach, no wary stalking of its prey. It was the man-eater, all right. Bisnu felt a cold shiver run down his spine. He felt a little sick.

The panther stood in the clearing with a slight thrusting forward of the head. This gave it the appearance of gazing intently and rather short-sightedly at some invisible object in the clearing. But there is nothing short-sighted about a panther's vision. Its sight and hearing are acute.

Bisnu remained motionless in the tree and sent up a prayer to all the gods he could think of. But the kid began bleating. The panther looked up and gave its deep-throated, rasping grunt—a fearsome sound, calculated to strike terror in any treeborne animal. Many a monkey, petrified by a panther's roar, has fallen from its perch to make a meal for Mr Spots. The man-eater was trying the same technique on Bisnu. But though the boy was trembling with fright, he clung firmly to the base of the spruce tree.

The panther did not make any attempt to leap into the tree. Perhaps, it knew instinctively that this was not the type of tree that it could climb. Instead, it described a semicircle round the tree, keeping its face turned towards Bisnu. Then it disappeared into the bushes.

The man-eater was cunning. It hoped to put the boy off his guard, perhaps entice him down from the tree. For, a few seconds later, with a half-humorous growl, it rushed back into the clearing and then stopped, staring up at the boy in some surprise. The panther was getting frustrated. It snarled, and putting its forefeet up against the tree trunk began scratching at the bark in the manner of an ordinary domestic cat. The tree shook at each thud of the beast's paw.

Bisnu began shouting for help.

The moon had not yet come up. Down in Manjari village, Bisnu's mother and sister stood in their lighted doorway, gazing anxiously up the pathway. Every now and then, Puja would turn to take a look at the small clock.

Sanjay's father appeared in a field below. He had a kerosene lantern in his hand.

'Sister, isn't your boy home as yet?' he asked.

'No, he hasn't arrived. We are very worried. He should have been home an hour ago. Do you think the panther will be about tonight? There's going to be a moon.'

'True, but it will be dark for another hour. I will fetch the other menfolk, and we will go up the mountain for your boy. There may have been a landslide during the rain. Perhaps the path has been washed away.'

'Thank you, brother. But arm yourselves, just in case the panther is about.'

'I will take my spear,' said Kalam Singh. 'I have sworn to spear that devil when I find him. There is some evil spirit dwelling in the beast and it must be destroyed!'

'I am coming with you,' said Puja.

'No, you cannot go,' said her mother. 'It's bad enough that Bisnu is in danger. You stay at home with me. This is work for men.'

'I shall be safe with them,' insisted Puja. 'I am going, Mother!' And she jumped down the embankment into the field and followed Sanjay's father through the village.

Ten minutes later, two men armed with axes had joined Kalam Singh in the courtyard of his house, and the small party moved silently and swiftly up the mountain path. Puja walked in the middle of the group, holding the lantern. As soon as the village lights were hidden by a shoulder of the hill, the men began to shout—both to frighten the panther, if it was about, and to give themselves courage.

Bisnu's mother closed the front door and turned to the image of Ganesha, the god for comfort and help.

Bisnu's calls were carried on the wind, and Puja and the men heard him while they were still half a mile away. Their own shouts increased in volume and, hearing their voices, Bisnu felt strength return to his shaking limbs. Emboldened by the approach of his own people, he began shouting insults at the snarling panther, then throwing twigs and small branches at the enraged animal. The kid added its bleats to the boy's shouts, the birds took up the chorus. The langoors squealed and grunted, the searchers shouted themselves hoarse, and the panther howled with rage. The forest had never before been so noisy.

As the search party drew near, they could hear the panther's savage snarls, and hurried, fearing that perhaps Bisnu had been seized. Puja began to run.

'Don't rush ahead, girl,' said Kalam Singh. 'Stay between us.'

The panther, now aware of the approaching humans, stood still in the middle of the clearing, head thrust forward in a familiar stance. There seemed too many men for one panther. When the animal saw the light of the lantern dancing between the trees, it turned, snarled defiance and hate, and without another look at the boy in the tree, disappeared into the bushes. It was not yet ready for a showdown.

VII

Nobody turned up to claim the little goat, so Bisnu kept it. A goat was a poor substitute for a dog, but, like Mary's lamb, it followed Bisnu wherever he went, and the boy couldn't help being touched by its devotion. He took it down to the stream, where it would skip about in the shallows and nibble the sweet grass that grew on the banks.

As for the panther, frustrated in its attempt on Bisnu's life, it did not wait long before attacking another human.

It was Chittru who came running down the path one afternoon, bubbling excitedly about the panther and the postman.

Chittru, deeming it safe to gather ripe bilberries in the daytime, had walked about half a mile up the path from the village, when he had stumbled across Mela Ram's mailbag lying on the ground. Of the postman himself there was no sign. But a trail of blood led through the bushes.

Once again, a party of men headed by Kalam Singh and accompanied by Bisnu and Chittru, went out to look for the postman. But though they found Mela Ram's bloodstained clothes, they could not find his body. The panther had made no mistake this time.

It was to be several weeks before Manjari had a new postman.

A few days after Mela Ram's disappearance, an old woman was sleeping with her head near the open door of her house. She had been advised to sleep inside with the door closed, but the nights were hot and anyway the old woman was a little deaf, and in the middle of the night, an hour before moonrise, the panther seized her by the throat. Her strangled cry woke her grown-up son, and all the men in the village woke up at his shouts and came running.

The panther dragged the old woman out of the house and down the steps, but left her when the men approached with their axes and spears, and made off into the bushes. The old woman was still alive, and the men made a rough stretcher of bamboo and vines and started carrying her up the path. But they had not gone far when she began to cough, and because of her terrible throat wounds, her lungs collapsed and she died.

It was the 'dark of the month'—the week of the new moon when nights are darkest.

Bisnu, closing the front door and lighting the kerosene lantern, said, 'I wonder where that panther is tonight!'

The panther was busy in another village: Sarru's village.

A woman and her daughter had been out in the evening bedding the cattle down in the stable. The girl had gone into the house and the woman was following. As she bent down to go in at the low door, the panther sprang from the bushes. Fortunately, one of its paws hit the doorpost and broke the force of the attack, or the woman would have been killed. When she cried out, the men came round shouting and the panther slunk off. The woman had deep scratches on her back and was badly shocked.

The next day, a small party of villagers presented themselves in front of the magistrate's office at Kemptee and demanded that something be done about the panther. But the magistrate was away on tour, and there was no one else in Kemptee who had a gun. Mr Nautiyal met the villagers and promised to write to a well-known shikari, but said that it would be at least a fortnight before the shikari would be able to come.

Bisnu was fretting because he could not go to school. Most boys would be only too happy to miss school, but when you are living in a remote village in the mountains and having an education is the only way of seeing the world, you look forward to going to school, even if it is five miles from home. Bisnu's exams were only two weeks off, and he didn't want to remain in the same class while the others were promoted. Besides, he knew he could pass even though he had missed a number of lessons. But he had to sit for the exams. He couldn't miss them.

'Cheer up, Bhaiya,' said Puja, as they sat drinking glasses of hot tea after their evening meal. 'The panther may go away once the rains break.'

'Even the rains are late this year,' said Bisnu. 'It's so hot and dry. Can't we open the door?'

'And be dragged down the steps by the panther?' said his mother. 'It isn't safe to have the window open, let alone the door.' And she went to the small window—through which a cat would have found difficulty in passing—and bolted it firmly.

With a sigh of resignation, Bisnu threw off all his clothes except his underwear and stretched himself out on the earthen floor.

'We will be rid of the beast soon,' said his mother. 'I know it in my heart. Our prayers will be heard, and you shall go to school and pass your exams.'

To cheer up her children, she told them a humorous story which had been handed down to her by her grandmother. It was all about a tiger, a panther and a bear, the three of whom were made to feel very foolish by a thief hiding in the hollow trunk of a banyan tree. Bisnu was sleepy and did not listen very attentively. He dropped off to sleep before the story was finished.

When he woke, it was dark and his mother and sister were asleep on the cot. He wondered what it was that had woken him. He could hear his sister's easy breathing and the steady ticking of the clock. Far away an owl hooted—an unlucky sign, his mother would have said; but she was asleep and Bisnu was not superstitious.

And then he heard something scratching at the door, and the hair on his head felt tight and prickly. It was like a cat scratching, only louder. The door creaked a little whenever it felt the impact of the paw—a heavy paw, as Bisnu could tell from the dull sound it made.

'It's the panther,' he muttered under his breath, sitting up on the hard floor.

The door, he felt, was strong enough to resist the panther's weight. And if he set up an alarm, he could rouse the village. But the middle of the night was no time for the bravest of men to tackle a panther.

In a corner of the room stood a long bamboo stick with a sharp knife tied to one end, which Bisnu sometimes used for spearing fish. Crawling on all fours across the room, he grasped the home-made spear, and then scrambling on to a cupboard, he drew level with the skylight window. He could get his head and shoulders through the window.

'What are you doing up there?' said Puja, who had woken up at the sound of Bisnu shuffling about the room.

'Be quiet,' said Bisnu. 'You'll wake Mother.'

Their mother was awake by now. 'Come down from there, Bisnu. I can hear a noise outside.'

'Don't worry,' said Bisnu, who found himself looking down on the wriggling animal which was trying to get its paw in under the door. With his mother and Puja awake, there was no time to lose. He had got the spear through the window, and though he could not manoeuvre it so as to strike the panther's head, he brought the sharp end down with considerable force on the animal's rump.

With a roar of pain and rage the man-eater leapt down from the steps and disappeared into the darkness. It did not pause to see what had struck it. Certain that no human could have come upon it in that fashion, it ran fearfully to its lair, howling until the pain subsided.

VIII

A panther is an enigma. There are occasions when it proves himself to be the most cunning animal under the sun, and yet the very next day it will walk into an obvious trap that no self-respecting jackal would ever go near. One day a panther will prove itself to be a complete coward and run like a hare from a couple of dogs, and the very next it will dash in amongst half a dozen men sitting round a camp fire and inflict terrible injuries on them.

It is not often that a panther is taken by surprise, as its power of sight and hearing are very acute. It is a master at the art of camouflage, and its spotted coat is admirably suited for the purpose. It does not need heavy jungle to hide in. A couple of bushes and the light and shade from surrounding trees are enough to make it almost invisible.

Because the Manjari panther had been fooled by Bisnu, it did not mean that it was a stupid panther. It simply meant that it had been a little careless. And Bisnu and Puja, growing in confidence since their midnight encounter with the animal, became a little careless themselves.

Puja was hoeing the last field above the house and Bisnu, at the other end of the same field, was chopping up several branches of green oak, prior to leaving the wood to dry in the loft. It was late afternoon and the descending sun glinted in patches on the small river. It was a time of day when only the most desperate and daring of man-eaters would be likely to show itself.

Pausing for a moment to wipe the sweat from his brow, Bisnu glanced up at the hillside, and his eye caught sight of a rock on the brown of the hill which seemed unfamiliar to him. Just as he was about to look elsewhere, the round rock began to grow and then alter its shape, and Bisnu watching in fascination was at last able to make out the head and forequarters of the panther. It looked enormous from the angle at which he saw it, and for a moment he thought it was a tiger. But Bisnu knew instinctively that it was the man-eater.

Slowly, the wary beast pulled itself to its feet and began to walk round the side of the great rock. For a second it disappeared and Bisnu wondered if it had gone away. Then it reappeared and the boy was all excitement again. Very slowly and silently the panther walked across the face of the rock until it was in direct line with the corner of the field where Puja was working.

With a thrill of horror Bisnu realized that the panther was stalking his sister. He shook himself free from the spell which had woven itself round him and shouting hoarsely ran forward.

'Run, Puja, run!' he called. 'It's on the hill above you!'

Puja turned to see what Bisnu was shouting about. She saw him gesticulate to the hill behind her, looked up just in time to see the panther crouching for his spring.

With great presence of mind, she leapt down the banking of the field and tumbled into an irrigation ditch.

The springing panther missed its prey, lost its foothold on the slippery shale banking and somersaulted into the ditch a few feet away from Puja. Before the animal could recover from its surprise, Bisnu was dashing down the slope, swinging his axe and shouting, *'Maro, maro!'* (Kill, kill!).

Two men came running across the field. They, too, were armed with axes. Together with Bisnu they made a half-circle around the snarling animal, which turned at bay and plunged at them in order to get away. Puja wriggled along the ditch on her stomach. The men aimed their axes at the panther's head, and Bisnu had the satisfaction of getting in a well-aimed blow between the eyes. The animal then charged straight at one of the men, knocked him over and tried to get at his throat. Just then Sanjay's father arrived with his long spear. He plunged the end of the spear into the panther's neck.

The panther left its victim and ran into the bushes, dragging the spear through the grass and leaving a trail of blood on the ground. The men followed cautiously—all except the man who had been wounded and who lay on the ground, while Puja and the other womenfolk rushed up to help him.

The panther had made for the bed of the stream and Bisnu, Sanjay's father and their companion were able to follow it quite easily. The water was red where the panther had crossed the stream, and the rocks were stained with blood. After they had gone downstream for about a furlong, they found the panther lying still on its side at the edge of the water. It was mortally wounded, but it continued to wave its tail like an angry cat. Then, even the tail lay still.

'It is dead,' said Bisnu. 'It will not trouble us again in this body.'

'Let us be certain,' said Sanjay's father, and he bent down and pulled the panther's tail.

There was no response.

'It is dead,' said Kalam Singh. 'No panther would suffer such an insult were it alive!'

They cut down a long piece of thick bamboo and tied the panther to it by its feet. Then, with their enemy hanging upside down from the bamboo pole, they started back for the village.

'There will be a feast at my house tonight,' said Kalam Singh. 'Everyone in the village must come. And tomorrow we will visit all the villages in the valley and show them the dead panther, so that they may move about again without fear.'

'We can sell the skin in Kemptee,' said their companion. 'It will fetch a good price.'

'But the claws we will give to Bisnu,' said Kalam Singh, putting his arm around the boy's shoulders. 'He has done a man's work today. He deserves the claws.'

A panther's or tiger's claws are considered to be lucky charms.

'I will take only three claws,' said Bisnu. 'One each for my mother and sister, and one for myself. You may give the others to Sanjay and Chittru and the smaller children.'

As the sun set, a big fire was lit in the middle of the village of Manjari and the people gathered round it, singing and laughing. Kalam Singh killed his fattest goat and there was meat for everyone.

IX

Bisnu was on his way home. He had just handed in his first paper, arithmetic, which he had found quite easy. Tomorrow it would be algebra, and when he got home he would have to practice square roots and cube roots and fractional coefficients.

Mr Nautiyal and the entire class had been happy that he had been able to sit for the exams. He was also a hero to them for his part in killing the panther. The story had spread through the villages with the rapidity of a forest fire, a fire which was now raging in Kemptee town.

When he walked past the hospital, he was whistling cheerfully. Dr Taylor waved to him from the verandah steps.

'How is Sanjay now?' she asked.

'He is well,' said Bisnu.

'And your mother and sister?'

'They are well,' said Bisnu.

'Are you going to get yourself a new dog?'

'I am thinking about it,' said Bisnu. 'At present I have a baby goat—I am teaching it to swim!'

He started down the path to the valley. Dark clouds had gathered and there was a rumble of thunder. A storm was imminent.

'Wait for me!' shouted Sarru, running down the path behind Bisnu, his milk pails clanging against each other. He fell into step beside Bisnu.

'Well, I hope we don't have any more man-eaters for some time,' he said. 'I've lost a lot of money by not being able to take milk up to Kemptee.'

'We should be safe as long as a shikari doesn't wound another panther. There was an old bullet wound in the man-eater's thigh. That's why it couldn't hunt in the forest. The deer were too fast for it.'

'Is there a new postman yet?'

'He starts tomorrow. A cousin of Mela Ram's.'

When they reached the parting of their ways, it had begun to rain a little.

'I must hurry,' said Sarru. 'It's going to get heavier any minute.'

'I feel like getting wet,' said Bisnu. 'This time it's the monsoon, I'm sure.'

Bisnu entered the forest on his own, and at the same time the rain came down in heavy opaque sheets. The trees shook in the wind and the langoors chartered with excitement.

It was still pouring when Bisnu emerged from the forest, drenched to the skin. But the rain stopped suddenly, just as the village of Manjari came into view. The sun appeared through a rift in the clouds. The leaves and the grass gave out a sweet, fresh smell.

Bisnu could see his mother and sister in the field transplanting the rice seedlings. The menfolk were driving the yoked oxen through the thin mud of the fields, while the children hung on to the oxen's tails, standing on the plain wooden barrows, and with weird cries and shouts sending the animals almost at a gallop along the narrow terraces.

Bisnu felt the urge to be with them, working in the fields. He ran down the path, his feet falling softly on the wet earth. Puja saw him coming and waved to him. She met him at the edge of the field.

'How did you find your paper today?' she asked.

'Oh, it was easy.' Bisnu slipped his hand into hers and together they walked across the field. Puja felt something smooth and hard against her fingers, and before she could see what Bisnu was doing, he had slipped a pair of bangles on her wrist.

'I remembered,' he said with a sense of achievement.

Puja looked at the bangles and burst out: 'But they are blue, Bhai, and I wanted red and gold bangles!' And then, when she saw him looking crestfallen, she hurried on: 'But they are very pretty and you did remember... Actually, they're just as nice as red and gold bangles! Come into the house when you are ready. I have made something special for you.'

'I am coming,' said Bisnu, turning towards the house. 'You don't know how hungry a man gets, walking five miles to reach home!'

MAN-EATER

Frank Buck with Edward Anthony

> Frank Buck spent a great many years collecting live wild animals for zoos, circuses, and dealers. He was famous for his early 'Bring 'em Back Alive' documentary films. In the following story he tells of the capture of a huge tiger at Johore, for an American zoo.

In 1926, I was again in Singapore putting the finishing touches to a splendid collection. My compound was fairly bursting with fine specimens. I had brought back from Siam a fine assortment of argus pheasants, fireback pheasants, and many small cage birds. Out of Borneo I had come with a goodly gang of man-like orang-utans and other apes. From Sumatra I had emerged with some fat pythons and a nice group of porcupines, binturongs, and civet cats. Celebes had yielded an imposing array of parrots, cockatoos, lories (brush-tongued parrots of a gorgeous colourings)—one of the biggest shipments of these birds I had ever made. My trip to Burmah was represented by a couple of black leopards (more familiarly known as panthers), several gibbons, and a sizeable army of small rhesus monkeys.

In addition, I had a number of other specimens picked up along the line.

I was to sail for San Francisco in a couple of weeks. This meant I would have to make a thorough inspection of my crates and cages to make sure they were all in shape to stand the rigours of a thirty-five or forty-day trip across the Pacific.

With Hin Mong, the Chinese carpenter who had served me for years, I made the rounds of the various boxes, and he made the notes of new cages and crates that were needed.

His cleverness knows no bounds. Working with a home-made saw, crude chisel made out of a scrap of iron shaped and sharpened on a grind-stone, and a few other primitive tools, he does carpentry that is as finished as if it came out of an up-to-date shop equipped with the finest of tools. Some of it, in fact, is finer than any carpenter work I have ever seen done anywhere. With a couple of chow-boys (apprentices) to assist him, Hin Mong would pitch into any task to which I assigned him and when it was done it was a piece of work to be proud of.

The owner of the house in Katong where I usually lived when in Singapore had sold it, making it necessary for me to move out, although I still maintained my compound there. After the sale of the house I invariably stayed at the Raffles Hotel in Singapore. I had just returned to my room there after an early morning session with Hin Mong, in the course of which we made a final inspection of the crates and cages, when I was informed that the Sultan of Johore was on the telephone and wished to speak to me at once. Whenever the Sultan telephoned, the information that he was on the wire was passed on to me with much ceremony, sometimes my good friend Aratoon, one of the owners of the hotel, announcing the news in person.

As the morning was still young I was puzzled, for it was

most unusual for H.H. to telephone so early. It was a very serious H.H. that spoke to me. He got to his business without any loss of time. Did I still want a man-eating tiger? Well, here was my chance. Breathlessly he told me that a coolie on a rubber plantation twenty-five miles north of Johore Bahru had been seized by a tiger while at work and killed. The animal, a man-eater, had devoured part of the body. Work, of course, was at a standstill on the plantation. The natives were in a state of terror. He (the Sultan) was sending an officer and eight soldiers to fight on the killer. It was necessary to show some action at once to ease the minds of his frightened subjects. If I thought I could catch the man-eater alive he would be glad to place the officer and soldiers under my command, with instructions to do my bidding. If, after looking over the situation, it became apparent that in trying to capture the killer alive, we were taking a chance of losing him, he expected me to have the beast immediately shot. He wanted no effort spared in locating the animal. There would be no peace in the minds and hearts of his subjects in the district where the outrage was committed until the cause was removed. In a series of crisp sentences the Sultan got the story off his chest. This was an interesting transition from his lighter manner, the vein in which I most frequently saw him.

Needless to say I leaped at the opportunity to try for a man-eater. H.H. asked me to join him at the fort over in Johore Bahru, which I agreed to do without delay.

At the fort, which is the military headquarters for the State to Johore, the Sultan introduced me to the officer he had selected to assist me, a major with a good record as a soldier and a hunter. He was a quiet little chap, so well-mannered that his courtesy almost seemed exaggerated. (The Malays, by the way, are the best-mannered people in Asia.) His soldiers were a likely looking contingent. It was obvious that H.H. had picked good men to help me with the job.

The major was not in uniform. He was dressed in ordinary rough clothes of European cut. I was interested in the rifle he carried. It was a Savage .303, which most hunters consider too small a gun for tiger-shooting. This capable Malay, however, had killed several tigers with this weapon, the Sultan told me.

The major's command were dressed in khaki shirts and 'shorts' affected by Malay soldiers. They wore heavy stockings that resembled golf hose. If not for the little black Mohammedan caps on their heads and their weapons—(each was armed with a big sword-like knife and a Malayan military rifle)—they might have been taken for a group of boy scouts. A cartridge-belt around each man's waist topped off the war-like note.

The major bowed two or three times and announced in his fairly good English that he was ready to start. We departed, the officer and his men piling into a small motor lorry, Ali and I following in my car. The asphalt roads of Johore are excellent—many of them were the work of American road-builders who did a wonderful job of converting stretches of wilderness into fine highways—and we were able to motor to within three miles of the killing. The rest of the journey we made on foot over a jungle trail.

I had requested the Sultan to order that the body of the slain coolie left where it was when the killer had finished his work. When we arrived we found a group of excited natives standing around the mangled remains. One leg had been eaten off to the thigh. The animal had also consumed the better part of one shoulder, and to give the job an added touch of thoroughness had gouged deeply into the back of the neck.

Other groups of natives were standing around not far

from the body, some of them hysterically jabbering away, some making weird moaning noises, others staring down at the ground in silence. One has to have a good comprehension of the wild world-old superstitions of these natives to appreciate fully what happens inside them when a man-eating tiger appears. All the fanaticism that goes with their belief in strange devils and ogres finds release when a tiger, their enemy of enemies, kills a member of their ranks. They act like a people who consider themselves doomed. Going into a delirium of fear that leaves them weak and spiritless, they become as helpless as little children. Under a strong leadership that suggests a grand unconcern about man-eating tigers, they can be rallied to work against the striped foe; but, until there are definite signs of a possible victory, this work is purely mechanical. The most casual glance reveals that each member of the terrified crew is staring hard at the jungle as he perfunctorily goes through the motions of doing whatever it is you assign him to.

An investigation revealed that the victim of the tiger had been working on a rubber tree when attacked. His tapping knife and latex cup (in which he caught the latex, or sap) were just where they had dropped from his hands when the poor devil was surprised, mute evidence of the suddenness of the assault. Then he had been dragged fifteen or twenty yards into some nearby brush.

Bordering along the jungle wall—as dense and black a stretch of jungle, incidentally, as I have ever seen—was a small pineapple plantation. This was not a commercial grove, but a modest affair cultivated by the estate coolies for their own use. An examination of the ground here revealed marks in the dirt that unmistakably were tiger tracks. The tiger's spoor led to a fence made by the natives to keep out wild pigs, whose fondness for pineapples had spelled the ruin of more than one plantation. Through a hole in this fence—which could have easily been made by the tiger or might have been there when he arrived, the work of some other animal—the killer's movements could, without the exercise of much ingenuity, be traced in the soft earth across the pineapple grove into the coal-black jungle some fifty yards away.

It is no news that a tiger, after gorging himself on his kill, will return to devour the unfinished remains of his feast. If there is no heavy brush within convenient reach he will camouflage those remains with leaves and anything else that is handy for his purpose and go off to his lair. Confident that he has covered his left-over skilfully enough to fool even the smartest of the vultures, jackals, hyenas, and wild dogs, he curls up and enjoys one of those wonderful long sleeps that always follow a good bellyful and which I have always believed to be as much a part of the joy of making a good kill as the actual devouring of it.

I felt, as I studied the situation, that when the tiger returned for the rest of his kill—assuming that this creature would follow regulation lines and re-visit the scene of the slaughter—he would again make use of that hole in the fence. It was a perfectly simple conclusion. Either the animal would not return at all or if he returned, he would re-travel his former route.

'*Changkuls! Changkuls! Changkuls!*' I yelled as soon as I decided on a course of action. A changkul is a native implement that is widely used on the rubber plantations. It is a combination of shovel and hoe. With the assistance of the major I managed to make it clear to the natives what it was I wanted them to do.

My plan was to dig a hole barely within the borders of the pineapple plantation, so close to the hole in the fence through which the tiger had travelled on his first visit that if he returned and used the same route he would go tumbling down a pit from which there was no return—except in a cage.

I specified a hole four feet by four feet at the surface. This was to be dug fourteen or fifteen feet deep, the opening widening abruptly at about the half-way mark until at the very bottom it was to be a subterranean room ten feet across.

Soon we had a sizable gang of natives working away with the *changkuls*. The helpful major, to whom I had given instructions for the pit that was now being dug, bowed a sporting acquiescence to my plan when I knew well that this accomplished shikari who had brought down many tigers was aching to go forth into the jungle in quest of the man-eater.

The digging of the pit finished, we covered the top with nipa palms. Then we made away with the pile of dirt we had excavated, scattering it at a distance so that the tiger, if *he returned*, would see no signs of fresh soil. The body was left where it was.

Ali then returned with me to Johore Bahru where I planned to stay overnight at the rest-house adjoining the United Service Club. Before leaving, I placed the soldiers on guard at the coolie lines with instructions to keep the natives within those lines.

The coolie lines on a rubber plantation correspond to the headquarters of a big ranch in this country. There is a row of shacks in which the natives live, a store where they buy their provisions, etc. My idea was to give the tiger every possible chance to return. Too much activity near the stretch of ground where the body lay might have made him overcautious.

Early the next morning the soldiers were to examine the pit. If luck was with us and the tiger was a prisoner, a Chinese boy on the estate who owned a bicycle that he had learned to ride at a merry clip was to head for the nearest military post—(there is a whole series of them, very few jungle crossroads in Johore being without one)—and notify the authorities who in turn would immediately communicate with the fort at Johore Bahru.

In the next morning no word had been received at the fort. At noon I drove back to the rubber plantation to see if there was anything I could do. The situation was unchanged. There was no signs of the tiger. No one had seen him, not even the most imaginative native with a capacity for seeing much that was not visible to the normal eye.

In the body of the mangled native was decomposing. Though I did not like to alter my original plan, I acquiesced when the natives appealed to me to let them give their fallen comrade a Mohammedan burial (the Malay version thereof). They put the body in a box and carried it off for interment.

The major did not conceal his desire to go off into the jungle with his men to seek the killer there. He was characteristically courteous, bowing politely as he spoke, and assuring me that he had nothing but respect for my plan. Yes, the luan's idea was a good one—doubtless, it might prove successful under different circumstances—but it was not meeting with any luck, and would I consider him too bold if he suggested beating about the nearby jungle with his men in an effort to trace the eater of the coolie?

What could I say? My plan had not accomplished anything and we were no closer to catching our man-eater than when we first got to work. I readily assented, stipulating only that the pit remained as it was, covered with nipa palms and ready for a victim—though if the animal returned after the number of hours that had elapsed, it would be performing freakishly.

There was no point in my staying there. So, when the major went off into the jungle with his men, I left the scene, returning to Singapore with Ali. I still had considerable work to do before the big collection of animals and birds in my compound would be ready for shipment to America.

I felt upset all the way back to Singapore. Here was the first chance I had ever had to take a man-eating tiger and I had failed. Perhaps I was not at fault—after all, the business of capturing animals is not an exact science—but just the same I was returning without my man-eater and I was bitterly disappointed. Ali did his best to cheer me up, but all he succeeded in doing was to remind me over and over again that I had failed. Using words sparingly and gestures freely, he tried to communicate the idea that after all a man could worry through life without a man-eating tiger. In an effort to change the expression on my face he grinned like an ape and made movements with his hands designed, I am sure, to convey the idea of gaiety. He was not helping a bit. Feeling that I was too strongly resisting his efforts to buck me up, he grew peeved and resorted to his old trick of wrinkling up his nose. This drew from me the first laugh I had had in several days. Seeing me laugh, Ali broke into a laugh too, wrinkling up his nose a few times more by way of giving me a thoroughly good time.

When we returned to Singapore I kept in touch with the situation by telephone, the fort reporting that though the major and his men had combed every inch of the jungle for some distance around, they found no trace of the killer. The major opined that the beast had undoubtedly left the district and that further search would accomplish nothing.

'Well, that's that,' I said to myself as I prepared to busy myself in the compound with the many tasks that were waiting for me there.

The third day, very early in the morning, just as I was

beginning to dismiss from my mind the events that had taken place on that rubber plantation, I received a telegram from the Sultan of Johore which, with dramatic suddenness, announced that the tiger had fallen into the pit! No one knew exactly when. 'Some time last night.' Would I hurry to the plantation with all possible haste? He had tried to reach me by phone but failed, so he had sent a fast telegram.

Would I? What a question! Perhaps it is unnecessary for me to say how delighted I was over the prospect of returning to the plantation to get my man-eating tiger. Ali ran me a close second, the old boy's joy (much of it traceable to my own, no doubt, for. Ali was usually happy when I was) being wonderful to behold.

We climbed into the car and set out for the plantation at a terrific clip. At least half the way we travelled at the rate of seventy miles an hour, very good work for the battered bus I was driving.

When we arrived, the natives were packed deep around the sides of the pit. Never have I witnessed such a change in morale. There was no suggestion of rejoicing—for the natives endow tigers with supernatural powers and they do not consider themselves safe in the presence of one unless he is dead or inside a cage—but they were again quick in their movements. A determined looking crew, they could now be depended upon for real assistance.

In addition to the crowd of coolies, the group near the pit included the major and his soldiers and a white man and his wife from a nearby plantation. The woman, camera in hand, was trying to take a picture. Even in the wilds of Johore one is not safe from invasion by those terrible amateurs to whom nothing means anything but the occasion for taking another picture. I distinctly recall that one of my first impulses on arriving on the scene was to heave the lady to the tiger and then toss in her chatterbox of a husband for good measure. This no doubt established a barbarous strain in me.

I ploughed my way through the crowd to the mouth of the pit. The natives had rolled heavy logs over the opening, driven heavy stakes and lashed the cover down with rattan.

'*Apa ini?*' I inquired. '*Apa ini?*' [What is this?]

'Oh, *tuan*! *Harimu besar*!' came the chorused reply, the gist of it being that our catch was a 'great, big, enormous tiger.' I loosened a couple of the logs, making an opening through which I could peer down into the pit. Stretching out on my stomach, I took a look at the prisoner below, withdrawing without the loss of much time when the animal, an enormous creature, made a terrific lunge upward, missing my face with his paw by not more than a foot.

This was all I needed to convince me that the natives had shown intelligence in covering the mouth of the pit with those heavy logs. I did not believe that the beast could have escaped if the covering was not there; yet he was of such a tremendous size that it was barely possible he could pull himself out by sinking his claws into the side of the pit after taking one of those well-nigh incredible leaps.

The business of getting that tiger out of the pit presented a real problem. This was due to his size. I had not calculated on a monster like this, a great cat that could leap upward to within a foot of the mouth of the pit.

Ordinarily it is not much of a job to get a tiger out of a pit. After baiting it with a couple of fresh killed chickens, a cage with a perpendicular slide door is lowered. An assistant holds a rope which when released drops the door and makes the tiger a captive as soon as he decides to enter the cage for the tempting morsels within, which he will do when he becomes sufficiently hungry. A variation on this procedure, though not as frequently used, is to lower a box without a bottom over the tiger. This is arduous labour, requiring plenty of patience, but it is a method that can be employed successfully when the circumstances are right. When you have the box over the tiger and it is safely weighted down, you drop into the pit, slip a sliding bottom under the box and yell to the boys overhead to haul away at the ropes.

It was obvious that neither of these methods would do in this case. I simply could not get around the fact that I had under-estimated the size of the man-eater and had not ordered a deep enough pit. Our catch was so big that if we lowered a box he could scramble to the top of it in one well-aimed leap and jump out of the hole in another. Ordinary methods would not do. They were too dangerous.

I finally hit upon a plan, and, as a good part of the morning was still ahead of us, I decided to tear back to Singapore for the supplies I needed and race back post-haste and get that striped nuisance out of the pit that day. I could not afford to spend much more time on the plantation. I had so much work waiting for me in connection with that big shipment I was taking to the United States.

My first move on arriving in Singapore was to get hold of Hin Mong and put him and his chow-boys to work at once on a special long, narrow box with a slide door at one end. When I left for my next stop, Mong and his boys had cast aside all other tasks and were excitedly yanking out lumber for my emergency order. Knowing this Chinese carpenter's fondness for needless little fancy touches, I assailed his ears before departing with a few emphatic words to the effect that this was to be a plain job and that he was not to waste any time on the frills so dear to his heart.

Leaving Mong I headed for the bazaars, where I bought three or four hundred feet of strong native rope made of jungle fibres. Next I went to the Harbour Works and borrowed a heavy block-and-tackle. Then I hired a motor truck.

When I added to this collection an ordinary Western lasso, which I learned to use as a boy in Texas, I was ready to return to the rubber plantation for my tiger. While on the subject of that lasso, it might be appropriate to point out that the public gave Buffalo Jones one long horse laugh when he announced his intention of going to Africa and roping big game, and that not long afterwards the laugh was on the public, for Buffalo serenely proceeded to do exactly what he said he would. I have never gone in for that sort of thing, but my rope, which is always kept handy, has been useful many times, even a crane, a valuable specimen, having been lassoed on the wing as it sailed out over the ship's side after a careless boy had left its shipping box open.

When the box was made—and though Hin Mong and his chow-boys threw it together hastily, it was a good strong piece of work—I loaded it and the coil of rope and the block-and-tackle on to the truck and sent this freight on its way to the rubber plantation, putting it in charge of Ali's nephew, who was then acting as his uncle's assistant at the compound. I gave him a driver and two other boys and sent them on their journey after Ali had given his nephew instructions on how to reach the rubber plantation. Four boys were needed to carry the supplies, three miles from the end of the road through the jungle trail to the plantation.

My own car, which had carried Ali and me on so many other important trips, carried us again. Our only baggage was my lasso, which I had dropped on the floor of this speedy but badly mutilated conveyance of mine that for want of a better name I called an automobile.

As I had not seen the Sultan since the day he turned his major and those eight soldiers over to me, I decided to drop in on him on the way to the rubber plantation.

Having learned he was at the fort, I headed for these glorified barracks, where H.H. greeted me effusively. He came out of the fort as we pulled up, leaning over the side of the car. He congratulated me a couple of times on my success in getting the tiger into the pit. Then, very solemnly—and for half a second I did not realise that he had reverted to his bantering manner—he said, 'Glad you stop here before you go to take the tiger from the pit. I would never forgive you if you do not say goodbye before the tiger eat you.'

Laughing, I told H.H., whose eyes were resting on the lasso at the bottom of the car, 'You don't seem very confident, do you?'

'Confident?' came the reply. 'Sure! You are going to catch the tiger with a rope like cowboy, no? Very simple, this method, no? Very simple. Why don't you try catch elephant this way too? Very simple.' Then the Sultan broke into one of those hearty roars of his, slapping his thighs as he doubled up with laughter.

'Don't you think I can do it, H.H.?' I asked.

Tactfully, he declined to answer with a yes or a no. All he said was, 'This is a tiger, not an American cow.' This was more eloquent than a dozen noes.

'I'll tell you what, H.H.,' I said. 'I'll make a little bet with you, just for the fun of it. I'll bet you a bottle of champagne that I'll have that tiger alive in Johore Bahru before the sun goes down.' H.H. never could be induced to make a wager for money with a friend; that's why I stipulated wine.

'I bet you,' he grinned. 'But how can I collect if the tiger eats you?' (Turning to Ali with mock sternness.) 'Ali, you do not forget that your tuan owes me a bottle champagne if he does not come back!' Then he exploded into another one of his body-shaking laughs.

We were off in a few minutes. Clouds were gathering overhead and it looked as if it was going to rain. I wanted to get my job over with before the storm broke. Stepping on the gas, I waved a good-bye to H.H., and we were on our way.

I was worried by the overcast skies, but I did not regard the impending storm as a serious obstacle. It looked like a 'Sumatra', a heavy rain and wind-storm of short duration, followed by bright sunshine that always seems freakish to those who do not know the East. The chief difficulty imposed by the storm, in the event that it broke, would be the slippery footing that would result. A secondary problem would be the stiffening of the ropes. Rope, when it has been well-exposed to rain, hardens somewhat, although it can be handled. If it rained, my job would be so much tougher.

We tore along at maximum speed, my engine heralding our approach all along the line with a mighty roar. Considering the terrific racket, I had a right to expect the speedometer to indicate a new speed record instead of a mere seventy an hour. My bus always got noisy when I opened her up, reminding me of a terrier trying to bark like a St. Bernard.

The skies grew darker as we raced along and when we were a short distance from the point where it was necessary to complete the journey on foot, a light rain started to fall. By the time we were half-way to the plantation it was raining hard and Ali and I were nicely drenched when we arrived.

The rain had driven many of the coolies to cover, but at least a score of them were still standing around when we pulled up. The major and his soldiers, soaked to the skin, stood by faithfully, the major even taking advantage of this inopportune moment to congratulate me again—he had done it before—on my trapping of the man-eater. I appreciated this sporting attitude after the failure of his search in the jungle. However, I did not feel very triumphant. The tough part of the job was ahead of me. Getting a tiger out of a pit into a cage in a driving rainstorm is dangerous, strenuous work.

I got busy at once. Taking out my knife, I began cutting my coil of native rope into extra nooses. Then I knocked aside some of the stakes that secured the pit's cover, rolled away some of the logs, and, stretching out flat with my head and shoulders extending out over the hole, began to make passes at the roaring enemy below with my lasso rope. One advantage of the rain was that it weakened the tiger's footing, making it impossible for him to repeat the tremendous leap upward he had made earlier in the day when I took my first look down the pit. As I heard him sloshing around in the mud and water at the bottom of his prison, I felt reassured. If the rain put me at a disadvantage, it did the same to the enemy also.

With the major standing by, rifle ready for action, I continued to fish for the tiger with my rope; the black skies giving me bad light by which to work. Once I got the lay of the land, I managed to drop the rope over the animal's head, but before I could pull up the slack—the rain had made the rope 'slow'—he flicked it off with a quick movement of the paw. A second time I got it over his head, but this time his problem was even easier for the forepart of the stiffening slack landed close enough to his mouth to enable him to bite the rope into two with one snap. Making a new loop in the lasso I tried over and over but he either eluded my throw or fought free of the noose with lightning-fast movements in which teeth and claws worked together in perfect coordination as he snarled his contempt for my efforts. The rain continued to come down in torrents. When it rains in Johore, it rains—an ordinary Occidental rainstorm being a mere sprinkle compared to an honest-to-goodness 'Sumatra'.

By now I was so thoroughly drenched that I no longer minded the rain on my body; it was only when the water dripped down into my eyes then I found myself growing irritated.

After working in this fashion for an hour till my shoulders ached from the awkward position I was in, I succeeded in looping a noose over the animal's head and through his mouth, using a fairly dry fresh rope that responded when I gave it a quick jerk. This accomplished my purpose, which was to draw the corners of his mouth inward so that his lips were stretched taut over his teeth, making it impossible for him to bite through the rope without biting through his lips. I yelled to the coolies who were standing by ready for action to tug away at the rope, which they did, pulling the crouching animal's head and forequarters clear of the bottom of the pit. This was the first good look at the foe I had had. The eyes hit me the hardest. Small for the enormous head, they glared an implacable hatred.

Quickly bringing another rope into play, I ran a second hitch around the struggling demon's neck, another group of coolies (also working under Ali's direction) pulling away at this rope from the side of the pit opposite the first ropehold. It was no trouble, with two groups of boys holding the animal's head and shoulders up, to loop a third noose under the forelegs and a fourth under the body. Working with feverish haste, I soon had eight different holds on the man-eater of Johore. With coolies tugging—away at each line, we pulled the monster up nearly even with the top of the pit and held him there. His mouth, distorted with rage plus what the first rope was doing to it, was a hideous sight. With hind legs he was thrashing away furiously, also doing his frantic best to get his roped forelegs into action.

I was about to order the lowering of the box when one of the coolies let out a piercing scream. He was the number one boy on the first rope. Looking around I saw that he had lost his footing in the slippery mud, and, in his frenzied efforts to save himself, was sliding head first for the mouth of the pit. I was in a position where I could grab him, but I went at it so hard that I lost my own footing and the two of us would have rolled over into the pit if Ali, who was following me around with an armful of extra nooses, hadn't quickly grabbed me and slipped one of these ropes between my fingers. With a quick tug, he and one of the soldiers pulled us out of danger.

The real menace, if the coolie and I had rolled over into the pit was that the other coolies would probably have lost their heads and let go the ropes. With them holding on there was no serious danger, for the tiger was firmly lashed.

I've wondered more than once what would have occurred if the native and I had gone splashing to the bottom of that hole. Every time I think of it, it gives me the creeps; for though the coolies at the ropes were dependable enough when their tuan was around to give them orders, they might easily have gone to pieces, as I've frequenly seen happen, had they suddenly decided that they were leaderless. It wouldn't have been much fun at the bottom of the pit with this brute of a tiger.

The coolies shrieked but they held. The rain continued to

come down in sheets and the ooze around the pit grew worse and worse. Self-conscious now about the slipperiness, the boys were finding it harder than ever to keep their feet.

The box would have to be lowered at once. With the tiger's head still almost even with the surface of the pit, we let the box down lengthwise, slide door end up. Unable to get too close, we had to manipulate the box with long poles. The hind legs had sufficient play to enable the animal to strike out with them, and time after time, after we painstakingly manoeuvred the cage into position with the open slide door directly under him, our enraged captive would kick it away. In the process the ropes gave a few inches, indicating that the strain was beginning to be too much for the boys. If we were forced to let the animal drop back after getting him to this point, it was a question if we'd ever be able to get him out alive.

Quickly I went over the situation with Ali. I was growing desperate. With the aid of the major and three of his soldiers we got the box firmly in place, the tired boys at the ropes responding to a command to tug away that lifted the animal a few inches above the point where his thrashing hind legs interfered with keeping it erect. I assigned the three soldiers to keep the box steady with poles which they braced against it. If we shifted the box again in the ooze we might lose our grip on it, so I cautioned them to hold it as it was.

'Major, I'm now leaving matters in your hands,' I said. 'See that the boys hold on and keep your rifle ready.' Before he had a chance to reply I let myself down into the pit, dodging the flying back feet. Covered with mud from head to foot as a result of my dropping into the slime, I grabbed the tiger by his tail, swung him directly over the opening of the box and fairly roared: 'Let go!' Let go they did, with me leaning on the box to help steady it.

The man-eater of Johore dropped with a bang to the bottom of Hin Mong's plainest box. I slid the door with a slam, leaned against it and bellowed for hammer and nails. I could feel the imprisoned beast pounding against the sides of his cell as he strove to free himself from the tangle of ropes around him. His drop, of necessity, had folded up his hind legs and I didn't see how he could right himself sufficiently in that narrow box for a lunge against the door at the top; but the brute weighed at least three hundred pounds, and if his weight shifted over against me he might, in my tired condition, knock me over and...

'Get the hammer and nails!' I screamed. 'Damn it, hurry up!' I leaned against the box with all my strength, pressing it against one side of the pit to hold the sliding door firmly closed.

No hammer! No nails!

Plastered with mud, my strength rapidly ebbing, I was in a fury over the delay.

'*Kasi pacoo*! [Bring nails!]' I shrieked in Malay, in case my English was not understood. 'Nails! Pacco! Nails' I cried. 'And a hammer, you helpless swine!' There weren't any swine present but that's what I called every one at the moment. I felt the tiger's weight shifting against me and I was mad with desperation.

The major yelled down that no one could find the nails. The can had been kicked over and the nails were buried in the mud. They had the hammer... Here it goes! I caught it... What the hell good is a hammer without nails?

'Give me nails, damn it, or I'll murder the pack of you!'

It was Ali who finally located the nails, buried in the mud, after what seemed like a week and was probably a couple of minutes. Over the side of the pit he scrambled to join me in a splash of mud. With a crazy feverishness I wielded the hammer while Ali held the nails in place, and at last Johore's coolie-killer was nailed down fast. Muffled snarls and growls of rage came through the crevices, left for breathing space.

Then I recall complaining to Ali that the storm must be getting worse. It was getting blacker. The tuan was wrong. The storm was letting up. Perhaps I mistook the mud that splashed over me as I fell to the floor of the pit, too weak to stand up, for extra heavy raindrops.

Ali lifted me to my feet and my brain cleared. I suddenly realized that the job was all done, that the man-eater of Johore was in that nailed-down box. I was overjoyed. Only a man in my field can fully realize the thrill I experienced over the capture of this man-eating tiger—the first, to my knowledge, ever brought to the United States.

Ropes were fastened around the box—(no one feared entering the pit now)—and with the aid of the block-and-tackle, our freight was hauled out of the hole.

Eight coolies were needed to get our capture back through the slime that was once a dry jungle trail to the highway leading to Johore Bahru. More than once they almost dropped their load, which they bore on carrying poles, as they skidded around in the three miles of sticky muck between the rubber plantation and the asphalt road which now reflected the sunlight, wistfully reappearing in regulation fashion after the rain and wind of the 'Sumatra'. There we loaded the box on to the waiting lorry, which followed Ali and me in my car.

About forty minutes later as the sun bathed the channel in the reddish glow of its vanishing rays, I planted the man-eater under the nose of the Sultan in front of the United Service Club in Johore Bahru.

With more mud on me than any one that ever stood at the

U.S.C.'s bar, I collected my bet, the hardest-earned champagne I ever tasted.

The Sultan was so respectful after I won this wager that once or twice I almost wished I hadn't caught his damned man-eater. H.H. is much more fun when he's not respectful. I enjoyed his pop-eyed felicitations but not nearly so much as some of the playful digs he has taken at me.

The man-eater of Johore, by the way, eventually wound up in the Longfellow Zoological Park, in Minneapolis, Minn.

THE CHAKRATA CAT

Ruskin Bond

The Chakrata is a small hill station roughly trek from one hill station to the other, sometimes alone, sometimes in company. It would take me about five days to cover the distance. I was a leisurely walker. You couldn't enjoy a like if you felt you had to catch a train at the end of it.

At Chakrata there was an old forest rest house where I would sometimes spend the night. Don't go looking for it now. It has fallen into disuse and been replaced by a new building closer to the tour.

Towards sunset, late that summer, I trudged upto the rest house and called out for the chowkidar. I forget his name. He was a grizelled old man, uncommunicative. If you told him you had just been chased by a bear, he would simply nod and say, 'You'd better rest, then. You must be tried,' Nothing about the bear!

Anyway, he opened up one of the bedrooms for me, prepared a modest meal (which I enjoyed, having eaten little all day), and offered to make a fire in the old fireplace.

Chakrata can be cold, even in September, and I offered to

pay for the firewood if he would fetch some. He switched on the bedroom and verandah lights and then walked to the rear of the building to fetch some wood.

That was when I saw the cat.

It was a large black cat, and it was sitting before the fireplace, almost as though expecting a fire to be lit. I hadn't noticed it entering the room, and it did not pay much attention to me, just kept strong into the fireplace. Then, when it heard the chowkidar returning, it got up and left the room.

'You have a cat?' I asked, trying to made conversation which he lit the fire.

He shook his head. 'Cats come for rats,' he said, which left me no wiser. And he took off, promising to bring me a cup of tea early next morning. There was a small bookshelf in a cover of room, and I found an old favourite, *A Working to the Curious* by M.R. James. This haunting stories of ghosts in old colleges kept me awake for a couple of hours; then I put out the light and got into bed.

I had forgotten about the cat.

Now I heard a soft purring as the cat jumped on to the bed and curled up near my feet. I am not particularly fond of cats, and my first impulse was to kick it off the bed. Then I thought, well, its probably used to sleeping in this room, especially with the fire lit. I'll let it be, as long as it doesn't start chasing rats in the middle of the night! And all it did was come a little closer to me, advancing from my feet to my knees, and purring loudly, as though quite satisfied with the situation.

I fell asleep and slept soundly. In fact, I must have slept for a couple of hours before I work to a feeling is wetness under my armpit. My vest was wet, and something was sucking away at my flesh.

It was with a feeling of horror that I realized that the cat had crawled into bed with me, that it was now stretched out beside me, and that it was licking away at my armpit with a certain amount of relish. For the purring was louder than ever.

I sat up in bed, flung the cat from me, and made a dash for the light switch. As the light came on, I saw the cat standing at the foot of the bed, tail erect and hair on end. It was very angry. And then, for the space of five seconds at the most, its appearance changed and its head was that of a human—a woman, black-browed with flaring nostrils and large crooked ears, her lips full and drenched with blood—my blood!

The moment passed and it was a cat's head once again. She let out a howl, strong from the bed, and disappeared through the bathroom door.

My shirt and vest were soaked with blood. For over an hour the cat had been licking and sucking at my fragile skin, wearing it away until the blood oozed out. Cat or vampire or witches revenant? Or a combination of all three.

I went to the bathroom. The cat had taken off through an open window. I closed the window, bathed my wound, examined myself in the mirror.

I had not been bitten. These were no teeth marks, no scratches. The tongue, and constant licking, had done the damage.

I found some cotton-wool in my haversacks, and used it to stop the trickle of blood from my armpit. Then I changed my vest and shirt, and sat down on an easy chair to wait for the down. It was three in the morning. I felt weak and fell asleep in my chair, to be wakened by the chowkidar knocking on my door with a cup of tea.

Chakrata is a lovely place, prettier than most hill stations, but I had no desire to stay any longer there. There was a bus to Dehradun at eight o'clock. I decided to cut short my trek and take the bus.

'Where's that cat of yours?' I asked the chowkidar before I left. He knew nothing about a cat. Did not care for cats. They were unlucky, the companions of evil spirits, creatures of the world of dead.

I did not stop to argue, but thanked him for his hospitality and took my leave.

The wound, if you can call it that, took some time to heal. The skin beneath my armpit was all crinkly for a few weeks, but the body heals itself, if given a chance to do so.

But what remains on my skin is a bright red mark, the size and shape of a cat's tongue. Its' been there all these years and won't go away. I'll show it to you, the next time you come to see me.

EYES OF THE CAT

Ruskin Bond

Her eyes seemed flecked with gold when the sun was on them. And as the sun set over the mountains, drawing a deep red wound across the sky, there was more than gold in Kiran's eyes. There was anger; for she had been cut to the quick by some remarks her teacher had made—the culmination of weeks of insults and taunts.

Kiran was poorer than most of the girls in her class and could not afford the tuitions that had become almost obligatory if one was to pass and be promoted. 'You'll have to spend another year in the ninth,' said Madam. 'And if you don't like that, you can find another school—a school where it won't matter if your blouse is torn and your tunic is old and your shoes are falling apart.' Madam had shown her large teeth in what was supposed to be a good-natured smile, and all the girls had tittered dutifully. Sycophancy had become part of the curriculum in Madam's private academy for girls.

On the way home in the gathering gloom, Kiran's two companions commiserated with her.

'She's a mean old thing,' said Aarti. 'She doesn't care for

anyone but herself.'

'Her laugh reminds me of a donkey braying,' said Sunita, who was more forthright.

But Kiran wasn't really listening. Her eyes were fixed on some point in the far distance, where the pines stood in silhouette against a night sky that was growing brighter every moment. The moon was rising, a full moon, a moon that meant something very special to Kiran, that made her blood tingle and her skin prickle and her hair glow and send out sparks. Her steps seemed to grow lighter, her limbs more sinewy as she moved gracefully, softly over the mountain path.

Abruptly she left her companions at a fork in the road.

'I'm taking the shortcut through the forest,' she said.

Her friends were used to her sudden whims. They knew she was not afraid of being alone in the dark. But Kiran's moods made them feel a little nervous, and now, holding hands, they hurried home along the open road.

The shortcut took Kiran through the dark oak forest. The crooked, tormented branches of the oaks threw twisted shadows across the path. A jackal howled at the moon; a nightjar called from urgency, and her breath came in short, sharp gasps. Bright moonlight bathed the hillside when she reached her home on the outskirts of the village.

Refusing her dinner, she went straight to her small room and flung the window open. Moonbeams crept over the windowsill and over her arms which were already covered with golden hair. Her strong nails had shredded the rotten wood of the windowsill.

Tail swishing and ears pricked, the tawny leopard came swiftly out of the window, crossed the open field behind the house, and melted into the shadows.

A little later it padded silently through the forest.

Although the moon shone brightly on the tin-roofed town, the leopard knew where the shadows were deepest and merged beautifully with them. An occasional intake of breath, which resulted in a short rasping cough, was the only sound it made.

Madam was returning from dinner at a ladies' club, called the Kitten Club as a sort of foil to the husbands' club affiliations. There were still a few people in the street, and while no one could help noticing Madam, who had the contours of a steam-roller, none saw or heard the predator who had slipped down a side alley and reached the steps of the teacher's house. It sat there silently, waiting with all the patience of an obedient schoolgirl.

When Madam saw the leopard on her steps, she dropped her handbag and opened her mouth to scream; but her voice would not materialize. Nor would her tongue ever be used again, either to savour chicken biryani or to pour scorn upon her pupils, for the leopard had sprung at her throat, broken her neck, and dragged her into the bushes.

In the morning, when Aarti and Sunita set out for school, they stopped as usual at Kiran's cottage and called out to her.

Kiran was sitting in the sun, combing her long black hair.

'Aren't you coming to school today, Kiran?' asked the girls.

'No, I won't bother to go today,' said Kiran. She felt lazy, but pleased with herself, like a contented cat.

'Madam won't be pleased,' said Aarti. 'Shall we tell her you're sick?'

'It won't be necessary,' said Kiran, and gave them one of her mysterious smiles. 'I'm sure it's going to be a holiday.'

TOOMAI OF THE ELEPHANTS

Rudyard Kipling

I will remember what I was. I am sick of rope and chain,
I will remember my old strength and all my forest aflairs.
I will not sell my back to man for a bundle of sugarcane,
I will go out to my own kind, and the wood-folk in their lairs.

I will go out until the day, until the morning break,
Out to the winds' untainted kiss, the waters' clean caress:
I will forget my ankle-ring and snap my picket-stake,
I will revisit my lost loves, and playmates masterless!

Kala Nag, which means Black Snake, had served the Indian government in every way that an elephant could serve it for forty-seven years, and as he was fully twenty years old when he was caught, that makes him nearly seventy—a ripe age for an elephant. He remembered pushing, with a big leather pad on his forehead, at a gun stuck in deep mud, and that was before the Afghan War of 1842, and he had not then come to his full strength. His mother, Radha Pyari—Radha the darling—

who had been caught in the same drive with Kala Nag, told him, before his little milk-tusks had dropped out, that elephants who were afraid always got hurt; and Kala Nag knew that the advice was good, for the first time that he saw a shell burst he backed, screaming, into a stand of piled rifles, and the bayonets pricked him in all his softest places. So, before he was twenty-five he gave up being afraid, and he was the best-loved and the best-looked-after elephant in the service of the Government of India. He had carried tents, twelve hundred pounds' weight of tents, on the march in Upper India; he had been hoisted into a ship at the end of a steam-crane and taken for days across the water, and made to carry a mortar on his back in a strange and rocky country very far from India, and had seen the Emperor Theodore lying dead in Magdala, and had come back again in the steamer, entitled, so the soldiers said, to the Abyssinian War Medal. He had seen his fellow elephants die of cold and epilepsy and starvation and sunstroke up at a place called Ali Masjid, ten years later; and afterwards he had been sent down thousands of miles south to haul and pile big baulks of teak in the timber-yards at Moulmein. There, he had half-killed an insubordinate young elephant who was shirking his fair share of the work.

After that he was taken off timber-hauling, and employed, with a few score of other elephants who were trained to the business, in helping to catch wild elephants among the Garo hills. Elephants are very strictly preserved by the Indian government. There is one whole department which does nothing else but hunt for them, and catch them, and break them in, and send them up and down the country as they are needed for work.

Kala Nag stood ten fair feet at the shoulders, and his tusks had been cut off short at five feet, and bound round the ends, to prevent them from splitting, with bands of copper; but he could do more with those stumps than any untrained elephant could do with the real sharpened ones.

When, after weeks and weeks of cautious driving of scattered elephants across the hills, the forty or fifty wild monsters were driven into the last stockade, and the big drop-gate, made of tree-trunks lashed together, jarred down behind them, Kala Nag, at the word of command, would go into that flaring, trumpeting pandemonium (generally at night, when the flicker of the torches made it difficult to judge distances), and, picking out the biggest and wildest tusker of the mob, would hammer him and hustle him into quiet while the men on the backs of the other elephants roped and tied the smaller ones.

There was nothing in the way of fighting that Kala Nag, the old wise Black Snake, did not know, for he had stood up more than once in his time to the charge of the wounded tiger, and, curling up his soft trunk to be out of harm's way, had knocked the springing brute sideways in mid-air with a quick sickle-cut of his head, that he had invented all by himself; had knocked him over, and knelt upon him with his huge knees till the life went out with a gasp and a howl, and there was only a fluffy striped thing on the ground for Kala Nag to pull by the tail.

'Yes,' said Big Toomai, his driver, the son of Black Toomai who had taken him to Abyssinia, and grandson of Toomai of the Elephants who had seen him caught, 'there is nothing that the Black Snake fears except me. He has seen three generations of us feed him and groom him, and he will live to see four.'

'He is afraid of me also,' said Little Toomai, standing up to his full height of four feet, with only one rag upon him. He was ten years old, the eldest son of Big Toomai, and, according to custom, he would take his father's place on Kala Nag's neck when he grew up, and would handle the heavy iron ankus, the elephant-goad that had been worn smooth by his father, and his grandfather, and his great-grandfather. He knew what he was talking of; for he had been born under Kala Nag's shadow, had played with the end of his trunk before he could walk, had taken him down to water as soon as he could walk, and Kala Nag would no more have dreamed of disobeying his shrill little orders than he would have dreamed of killing him on that day when Big Toomai carried the little brown baby under Kala Nag's tusks, and told him to salute his master that was to be.

'Yes,' said Little Toomai, 'he is afraid of me,' and he took long strides up to Kala Nag, called him a fat old pig, and made him lift up his feet one after the other.

'Wah!' said Little Toomai, 'thou art a big elephant,' and he wagged his fluffy head, quoting his father. 'The Government may pay for elephants, but they belong to us mahouts. When thou art old, Kala Nag, there will come some rich Rajah, and he will buy thee from the Government, on account of thy size and thy manners, and then thou wilt have nothing to do but to carry gold earrings in thy ears, and a gold howdah on thy back, and a red cloth covered with gold on thy sides, and walk at the head of the processions of the King. Then, I shall sit on thy neck, O Kala Nag, with a silver ankus, and men will run before us with golden sticks, crying, 'Room for the King's elephant!' That will be good, Kala Nag, but not so good as this hunting in the jungles.'

'Umph!' said Big Toomai. 'Thou art a boy, and as wild as a buffalo-calf. This running up and down among the hills is not the best Government service. I am getting old, and I do not love wild elephants. Give me brick elephant-lines, one stall to each elephant, and big stumps to tie them to safely, and flat, broad roads to exercise upon, instead of this come-and-go camping. Aha, the Cawnpore barracks were good. There was a bazaar close by, and only three hours' work a day.'

Little Toomai remembered the Cawnpore elephant-lines and said nothing. He very much preferred the camp life, and hated those broad, flat roads, with the daily grubbing for grass in the forage-reserve, and the long hours when there was nothing to do except to watch Kala Nag fidgeting in his pickets.

What Little Toomai liked was the scramble up bridle-paths that only an elephant could take; the dip into the valley below; the glimpses of the wild elephants browsing miles away; the rush of the frightened pig and peacock under Kala Nag's feet; the blinding warm rains, when all the hills and valleys smoked; the beautiful misty mornings when nobody knew where they would camp that night; the steady, cautious drive of the wild elephants, and the mad rush and blaze and hullabaloo of the last night's drive, when the elephants poured into the stockade like boulders in a landslide, found that they could not get out, and flung themselves at the heavy posts only to be driven back by yells and flaring torches and volleys of blank cartridge.

Even a little boy could be of use there, and Toomai was as useful as three boys. He would get his torch and wave it, and yell with the best. But the really good time came when the driving out began, and the Keddah—that is, the stockade—looked like a picture of the end of the world, and men had to make signs to one another, because they could not hear themselves speak. Then, Little Toomai would climb up to the top of one of the quivering stockade-posts, his sun-bleached brown hair flying loose all over his shoulders, and he looking like a goblin in the torch-light; and as soon as there was a lull you could hear his high-pitched yells of encouragement to Kala

Nag, above the trumpeting and crashing, and snapping of ropes, and groans of the tethered elephants. '*Mail, mail, Kala Nag*! (Go on, go on, Black Snake!) *Dani do*! (Give him the tusk!) *Somalol Somalol* (Careful, careful!) *Mara*! *Mara*! (Hit him, hit him!) Mind the post! *Arré*! *Arré*! *Hai*! *Yai*! *Kya-a-ah*!' he would shout, and the big fight between Kala Nag and the wild elephant would sway to and fro across the Keddah, and the old elephant-catchers would wipe the sweat out of their eyes, and find time to nod to Little Toomai wriggling with joy on the top of the posts.

He did more than wriggle. One night, he slid down from the post and slipped in between the elephants, and threw up the loose end of a rope, which had dropped, to a driver who was trying to get a purchase on the leg of a kicking young calf (calves always give more trouble than full-grown animals). Kala Nag saw him, caught him in his trunk, and handed him up to Big Toomai, who slapped him then and there, and put him back on the post.

Next morning he gave him a scolding, and said: 'Are not good brick elephant-lines and a little tent-carrying enough, that thou must needs go elephant-catching on thy own account, little worthless? Now those foolish hunters, whose pay is less than my pay, have spoken to Petersen Sahib of the matter.' Little Toomai was frightened. He did not know much of white men, but Petersen Sahib was the greatest white man in the world to him. He was the head of all the Keddah operations—the man who caught all the elephants for the Government of India, and who knew more about the ways of elephants than any living man.

'What...what will happen?' said Little Toomai.

'Happen! the worst that can happen. Petersen Sahib is a madman. Else, why should he go hunting these wild devils?

He may even require thee to be an elephant-catcher, to sleep anywhere in these fever—filled jungles, and at last to be trampled to death in the Keddah. It is well that this nonsense ends safely. Next week the catching is over, and we of the plains are sent back to our stations. Then, we will march on smooth roads, and forget all this hunting. But, son, I am angry that thou shouldst meddle in the business that belongs to these dirty Assamese jungle-folk. Kala Nag will obey none but me, so I must go with him into the Keddah; but he is only a fighting elephant, and he does not help to rope them. So, I sit at my ease, as befits a mahout—not a mere hunter—a mahout, I say, and a man who gets a pension at the end of his service. Is the family of Toomai of the Elephants to be trodden underfoot in the dirt of a Keddah? Bad one! Wicked one! Worthless son! Go and wash Kala Nag and attend to his ears, and see that there are no thorns in his feet; or else Petersen Sahib will surely catch thee and make thee a wild hunter—a follower of elephants' foot-tracks, a jungle-bear. Bah! Shame! Go!'

Little Toomai went off without saying a word, but he told Kala Nag all his grievances while he was examining his feet. 'No matter,' said Little Toomai, turning up the fringe of Kala Nag's huge right ear. 'They have said my name to Petersen Sahib, and perhaps—and perhaps—and perhaps—who knows? Hai! That is a big thorn that I have pulled out!'

The next few days were spent in getting the elephants together, in walking the newly caught wild elephants up and down between a couple of tame ones, to prevent them from giving too much trouble on the downward march to the plains, and in taking stock of the blankets and ropes and things that had been worn out or lost in the forest.

Petersen Sahib came in on his clever she-elephant Pudmini.

He had been paying off other camps among the hills, for the season was coming to an end, and there was a native clerk sitting at a table under a tree to pay the drivers their wages. As each man was paid he went back to his elephant, and joined the line that stood ready to start. The catchers, and hunters, and beaters, the men of the regular Keddah, who stayed in the jungle year in and year out, sat on the backs of the elephants that belonged to Petersen Sahib's permanent force, or leaned against the trees with their guns across their arms, and made fun of the drivers who were going away, and laughed when the newly caught elephants broke the line and ran about.

Big Toomai went up to the clerk with Little Toomai behind him, and Machua Appa, the head-tracker, said in an undertone to a friend of his, 'There goes one piece of good elephant-stuff at least. 'Tis a pity to send that young jungle-cock to moult in the plains.'

Now Petersen Sahib had ears all over him, as a man must have who listens to the most silent of all living things—the wild elephant. He turned where he was lying all along on Pudmini's back, and said, 'What is that? I did not know of a man among the plains—drivers who had wit enough to rope even a dead elephant.'

'This is not a man, but a boy. He went into the Keddah at the last drive, and threw Barmao there the rope when we were trying to get that young calf with the blotch on his shoulder away from his mother.'

Machua Appa pointed at Little Toomai, and Petersen Sahib looked, and Little Toomai bowed to the earth.

'He threw a rope? He is smaller than a picket-pin. Little one, what is thy name?' said Petersen Sahib.

Little Toomai was too frightened to speak, but Kala Nag

was behind him, and Toomai made a sign with his hand, and the elephant caught him up in his trunk and held him level with Pudmini's forehead, in front of the great Petersen Sahib. Then, Little Toomai covered his face with his hands, for he was only a child, and except where elephants were concerned, he was just as bashful as a child could be.

'Oho!' said Petersen Sahib, smiling underneath his moustache, 'and why didst thou teach thy elephant that trick? Was it to help thee steal green corn from the roofs of the houses when the ears are put out to dry?'

'Not green corn, Protector of the Poor—melons,' said Little Toomai, and all the men sitting about broke into a roar of laughter. Most of them had taught their elephants that trick when they were boys. Little Toomai was hanging eight feet up in the air, and he wished very much that he were eight feet under ground.

'He is Toomai, my son, Sahib,' said Big Toomai, scowling. 'He is a very bad boy, and he will end in a jail, Sahib.'

'Of that I have my doubts,' said Petersen Sahib. 'A boy who can face a full Keddah at his age does not end up in jails. See, little one, here are four annas to spend in sweetmeats because thou hast a little head under that great thatch of hair. In time thou mayest become a hunter, too.' Big Toomai scowled more than ever. 'Remember, though, that Keddahs are not good for children to play in,' Petersen Sahib went on.

'Must I never go there, Sahib?' asked Little Toomai, with a big gasp.

'Yes.' Petersen Sahib smiled again. 'When thou hast seen the elephants dance. That is the proper time. Come to me when thou hast seen the elephants dance, and then I will let thee go into all the Keddahs.'

There was another roar of laughter, for that is an old joke among elephant-catchers, and it means just never. There are great cleared flat places hidden away in the forests that are called elephants' ball-rooms, but even these are only found by accident, and no man has ever seen the elephants dance. When a driver boasts of his skill and bravery the other drivers say, 'And when didst *thou* see the elephants dance?'

Kala Nag put Little Toomai down, and he bowed to the earth again and went away with his father, and gave the silver four-anna piece to his mother, who was nursing his baby brother, and they all were put on Kala Nag's back, and the line of grunting, squealing elephants rolled down the hill-path to the plains. It was a very lively march on account of the new elephants, who gave trouble at every ford, and who needed coaxing or beating every other minute.

Big Toomai prodded Kala Nag spitefully, for he was very angry, but Little Toomai was too happy to speak. Petersen Sahib had noticed him, and given him money, so he felt as a private soldier would feel if he had been called out of the ranks and praised by his commander-in-chief.

'What did Petersen Sahib mean by the elephant-dance?' he said, at last, softly to his mother.

Big Toomai heard him and grunted. 'That thou shouldst never be one of these hill-buffaloes of trackers. *That* was what he meant. Oh, you in front, what is blocking the way?'

An Assamese driver, two or three elephants ahead, turned round angrily, crying: 'Bring up Kala Nag, and knock this youngster of mine into good behaviour. Why should Petersen Sahib have chosen *me* to go down with you donkeys of the rice-fields? Lay your beast alongside, Toomai, and let him prod with his tusks. By all the Gods of the Hills, these new elephants are possessed, or else they can smell their companions in the jungle.'

Kala Nag hit the new elephant in the ribs and knocked the wind out of him, as Big Toomai said, 'We have swept the hills of wild elephants at the last catch. It is only your carelessness in driving. Must I keep order along the whole line?'

'Hear him!' said the other driver. '*We* have swept the hills! Ho! ho! You are very wise, you plains-people. Anyone but a mud-head who never saw the jungle would know that *they* know that the drives are ended for the season. Therefore, all the wild elephants tonight will—but why should I waste wisdom on a river-turtle?'

'What will they do?' Little Toomai called out.

'Ohé, little one. Art thou there? Well, I will tell thee, for thou hast a cool head. They will dance, and it behoves thy father, who has swept *all* the hills of *all* the elephants, to double-chain his pickets tonight.'

'What talk is this?' said Big Toomai. 'For forty years, father and son, we have tended elephants, and we have never heard such moonshine about dances.'

'Yes; but a plains-man who lives in a hut knows only the four walls of his hut. Well, leave thy elephants unshackled tonight and see what comes; as for their dancing, I have seen the place where—*Bapree-Bap!* how many windings has the Dihang River? Here is another ford, and we must swim the calves. Stop still, you behind there.'

And in this way, talking and wrangling and splashing through the rivers, they made their first march to a sort of receiving-camp for the new elephants; but they lost their tempers long before they got there.

Then, the elephants were chained by their hind legs to their big stumps of pickets, and extra ropes were fitted to the new elephants, and the fodder was piled before them, and the hill-drivers went back to Petersen Sahib through the afternoon light, telling the plains-drivers to be extra careful that night, and laughing when the plains-drivers asked the reason.

Little Toomai attended to Kala Nag's supper, and as evening fell wandered through the camp, unspeakably happy, in search of a tom-tom. When an Indian child's heart is full, he does not run about and make a noise in an irregular fashion. He sits down to a sort of revel all by himself. And Little Toomai had been spoken to by Petersen Sahib! If he had not found what he wanted, I believe he would have burst. But the sweetmeat-seller in the camp lent him a little tom-tom—a drum beaten with the flat of the hand—and he sat down, cross-legged, before Kala Nag as the stars began to come out, the tom-tom in his lap, and he thumped and he thumped and he thumped, and the more he thought of the great honour that had been done to him, the more he thumped, all alone among the elephant-fodder. There was no tune and no words, but the thumping made him happy.

The new elephants strained at their ropes, and squealed and trumpeted from time to time, and he could hear his mother in the camp hut putting his small brother to sleep with an old, old song about the great God Shiv, who once told all the animals what they should eat. It is a very soothing lullaby, and the first verse says:

> Shiv, who poured the harvest and made the winds to blow,
> Sitting at the doorways of a day of long ago.
> Gave to each his portion, food and toil and fate,
> From the King upon the guddee to the Beggar at the gate.
> All things made he—Shiva the Preserver.

Mahadeo! Mahadeo! He made all—
Thorn for the camel, fodder for the kine.
And mothers heart for sleepy head, O little son of mine!

Little Toomai came in with a joyous tunk-a-tunk at the end of each verse, till he felt sleepy and stretched himself on the fodder at Kala Nag's side.

At last, the elephants began to lie down one after another, as is their custom, till only Kala Nag at the right of the line was left standing up; and he rocked slowly from side-to-side, his ears put forward to listen to the night wind as it blew very slowly across the hills. The air was full of all the night noises that, taken together, make one big silence—the click of one bamboo-stem against the other, the rustle of something alive in the undergrowth, the scratch and squawk of a half-waked bird (birds are awake in the night much more often than we imagine), and the fall of water ever so far away. Little Toomai slept for some time, and when he waked it was brilliant moonlight, and Kala Nag was still standing up with his ears cocked. Little Toomai turned, rustling in the fodder, and watched the curve of his big back against half the stars in heaven; and while he watched he heard, so far away that it sounded no more than a pinhole of noise pricked through the stillness, the 'hoot-toot' of a wild elephant.

All the elephants in the lines jumped up as if they had been shot, and their grunts at last waked the sleeping mahouts, and they came out and drove in the picket-pegs with big mallets, and tightened this rope and knotted that till all was quiet. One new elephant had nearly grubbed up his picket, and Big Toomai took off Kala Nag's leg-chain and shackled that elephant forefoot to hind-foot, but slipped a loop of grass-string round Kala

Nag's leg, and told him to remember that he was tied fast. He knew that he and his father and his grandfather had done the very same thing hundreds of times before. Kala Nag did not answer to the order by gurgling, as he usually did. He stood still, looking out across the moonlight, his head a little raised, and his ears spread like fans, up to the great folds of the Garo Hills.

'Look to him if he grows restless in the night,' said Big Toomai to Little Toomai, and he went into the hut and slept. Little Toomai was just going to sleep, too, when he heard the coir string snap with a little 'tang,' and Kala Nag rolled out of his pickets as slowly and as silently as a cloud rolls out of the mouth of a valley. Little Toomai pattered after him, barefooted, down the road in the moonlight, calling under his breath, 'Kala Nag! Kala Nag! Take me with you, O Kala Nag!' The elephant turned without a sound, took three strides back to the boy in the moonlight, put down his trunk, swung him up to his neck, and almost before Little Toomai had settled his knees slipped into the forest.

There was one blast of furious trumpeting from the lines, and then the silence shut down on everything, and Kala Nag began to move. Sometimes, a tuft of high grass washed along his sides as a wave washes along the sides of a ship, and sometimes a cluster of wild-pepper vines would scrape along his back, or a bamboo would creak where his shoulder touched it; but between those times he moved absolutely without any sound, drifting through the thick Garo forest as though it had been smoke. He was going uphill, but though Little Toomai watched the stars in the rifts of the trees, he could not tell in what direction.

Then, Kala Nag reached the crest of the ascent and stopped for a minute, and Little Toomai could see the tops of the trees lying all speckled and furry under the moonlight for miles and miles, and the blue-white mist over the river in the hollow. Toomai leaned forward and looked, and he felt that the forest was awake below him—awake and alive and crowded. A big brown fruit-eating bat brushed past his ear; a porcupine's quills rattled in the thicket; and in the darkness between the tree-stems he heard a hog-bear digging hard in the moist, warm earth, and snuffing as it digged.

Then, the branches closed over his head again, and Kala Nag began to go slowly down into the valley—not quietly this time, but as a runaway gun goes down a steep bank—in one rush. The huge limbs moved as steadily as pistons, eight feet to each stride, and the wrinkled skin of the elbow-points rustled. The undergrowth on either side of him ripped with a noise like torn canvas, and the saplings that he heaved away right and left with his shoulders sprang back again, and banged him on the flank, and great trails of creepers, all matted together, hung from his tusks as he threw his head from side-to-side and ploughed out his pathway. Then, Little Toomai laid himself down close to the great neck, lest a swinging bough should sweep him to the ground, and he wished that he were back in the lines again.

The grass began to get squashy, and Kala Nag's feet sucked and squelched as he put them down, and the night mist at the bottom of the valley chilled Little Toomai. There was a splash and a trample, and the rush of running water, and Kala Nag strode through the bed of a river, feeling his way at each step. Above the noise of the water, as it swirled round the elephant's legs, Little Toomai could hear more splashing and some trumpeting both up stream and down—great grunts and angry snortings, and all the mist about him seemed to be full of rolling, wavy shadows.

'Ai!' he said, half-aloud, his teeth chattering. 'The elephant-folk are out tonight. It is the dance, then.'

Kala Nag swashed out of the water, blew his trunk clear, and began another climb; but this time he was not alone, and he had not to make his path. That was made already, six feet wide, in front of him, where the bent jungle-grass was trying to recover itself and stand up. Many elephants must have gone that way only a few minutes before. Little Toomai looked back, and behind him a great wild tusker, with his little pig's eyes glowing like hot coals, was just lifting himself out of the misty river. Then the trees closed up again, and they went on and up, with trumpetings and crashings, and the sound of breaking branches on every side of them.

At last, Kala Nag stood still between two tree-trunks at the very top of the hill. They were part of a circle of trees that grew round an irregular space of some three or four acres, and in all that space, as Little Toomai could see, the ground had been trampled down as hard as a brick floor. Some trees grew in the centre of the clearing, but their bark was rubbed away, and the white wood beneath showed all shiny and polished in the patches of moonlight. There were creepers hanging from the upper branches, and the bells of the flowers of the creepers, great waxy white things like convolvuluses, hung down fast asleep; but within the limits of the clearing there was not a single blade of green—nothing but the trampled earth.

The moonlight showed it all iron-grey, except where some elephants stood upon it, and their shadows were inky black. Little Toomai looked, holding his breath, with his eyes starting out of his head, and as he looked, more and more and more elephants swung out into the open from between the tree-trunks. Little Toomai could count only up to ten, and he counted again and again on his fingers till he lost count of the tens, and his head began to swim. Outside the clearing he could hear them crashing in the undergrowth as they worked their way up the hillside; but as soon as they were within the circle of the tree-trunks they moved like ghosts.

There were white-tusked wild males, with fallen leaves and nuts and twigs lying in the wrinkles of their necks and the folds of their ears; fat, slow-footed she-elephants, with restless little pinky-black calves only three or four feet high running under their stomachs; young elephants with their tusks just beginning to show, and very proud of them; lanky, scraggy old-maid elephants, with their hollow, anxious faces, and trunks like rough bark; savage old bull-elephants, scarred from shoulder to flank with great weals and cuts of bygone fights, and the caked dirt of their solitary mud-baths dropping from their shoulders; and there was one with a broken tusk and the marks of the full-stroke, the terrible drawing scrape, of a tiger's claws on his side.

They were standing head to head, or walking to and fro across the ground in couples, or rocking and swaying all by themselves—scores and scores of elephants.

Toomai knew that, so long as he lay still on Kala Nag's neck, nothing would happen to him; for even in the rush and scramble of a Keddah-drive a wild elephant does not reach up with his trunk and drag a man off the neck of a tame elephant; and these elephants were not thinking of men that night. Once they started and put their ears forward when they heard the chinking of a leg-iron in the forest, but it was Pudmini, Petersen Sahib's pet elephant, her chain snapped short off, grunting, snuffling up the hillside. She must have broken her pickets, and come straight from Petersen Sahib's camp; and Little Toomai saw another elephant, one that he did not know, with deep rope-galls on his back and breast. He, too, must have run away from some camp in the hills about.

At last, there was no sound of any more elephants moving in the forest, and Kala Nag rolled out from his station between the trees and went into the middle of the crowd, clucking and gurgling, and all the elephants began to talk in their own tongue, and to move about.

Still lying down, Little Toomai looked down upon scores and scores of broad backs, and wagging ears, and tossing trunks, and little rolling eyes. He heard the click of tusks as they crossed other tusks by accident, and the dry rustle of trunks twined together, and the chafing of enormous sides and shoulders in the crowd, and the incessant flick and hissh of the great tails. Then, a cloud came over the moon, and he sat in black darkness; but the quiet, steady hustling and pushing and gurgling went on just the same. He knew that there were elephants all around Kala Nag, and that there was no chance of backing him out of the assembly; so he set his teeth and shivered. In a Keddah at least there was torchlight and shouting, but here he was all alone in the dark, and once a trunk came up and touched him on the knee.

Then an elephant trumpeted, and they all took it up for five or ten terrible seconds. The dew from the trees above spattered down like rain on the unseen backs, and a dull booming noise began, not very loud at first, and Little Toomai could not tell what it was; but it grew and grew, and Kala Nag lifted up one fore—foot and then the other, and brought them down on the ground—one-two, one-two, as steadily as trip-hammers. The elephants were stamping all together now, and it sounded like a war-drum beaten at the mouth of a cave. The dew fell from the trees till there was no more left to fall, and the booming went on, and the ground rocked and shivered, and Little Toomai put his hands up to his ears to shut out the sound. But it was all one gigantic jar that ran through him—this stamp of hundreds of heavy feet on the raw earth. Once or twice he could feel Kala Nag and all the others surge forward a few strides, and the thumping would change to the crushing sound of juicy green things being bruised, but in a minute or two the boom of feet on hard earth began again. A tree was creaking and groaning somewhere near him. He put out his arm and felt the bark, but Kala Nag moved forward, still tramping, and he could not tell where he was in the clearing. There was no sound from the elephants, except once, when two or three little calves squeaked together. Then he heard a thump and a shuffle, and the booming went on. It must have lasted fully two hours, and Little Toomai ached in every nerve; but he knew by the smell of the night air that the dawn was coming.

The morning broke in one sheet of pale yellow behind the green hills, and the booming stopped with the first ray, as though the light had been an order. Before Little Toomai had got the ringing out of his head, before even he had shifted his position, there was not an elephant in sight except Kala Nag, Pudmini, and the elephant with the rope-galls, and there was neither sign nor rustle nor whisper down the hillsides to show where the others had gone.

Little Toomai stared again and again. The clearing, as he remembered it, had grown in the night. More trees stood in the middle of it, but the undergrowth and the jungle-grass at the sides had been rolled back. Little Toomai stared once more. Now, he understood the trampling. The elephants had stamped out more room—had stamped the thick grass and juicy cane to trash, the trash into slivers, the slivers into tiny fibres, and the fibres into hard earth.

'Wah!' said Little Toomai, and his eyes were very heavy. 'Kala Nag, my lord, let us keep by Pudmini and go to Petersen Sahib's camp, or I shall drop from thy neck.'

The third elephant watched the two go away, snorted, wheeled round, and took his own path. He may have belonged to some little native king's establishment, fifty or sixty or a hundred miles away.

Two hours later, as Petersen Sahib was eating early breakfast, the elephants, who had been double-chained that night, began to trumpet, and Pudmini, mired to the shoulders, with Kala Nag, very foot-sore, shambled into the camp.

Little Toomai's face was grey and pinched, and his hair was full of leaves and drenched with dew; but he tried to salute Petersen Sahib, and cried faintly: 'The dance—the elephant-dance! I have seen it, and—I die!' As Kala Nag sat down, he slid off his neck in a dead faint.

But, since native children have no nerves worth speaking of, in two hours he was lying very contentedly in Petersen Sahib's hammock with Petersen Sahib's shooting-coat under his head, and a glass of warm milk, a little brandy, with a dash of quinine inside of him; and while the old hairy, scarred hunters of the jungles sat three-deep before him, looking at him as though he were a spirit, he told his tale in short words, as a child will, and wound up with:

'Now, if I lie in one word, send men to see, and they will find that the elephant-folk have trampled down more room in their dance-room, and they will find ten and ten, and many times ten, tracks leading to that dance-room. They made more room with their feet. I have seen it. Kala Nag took me, and I saw. Also, Kala Nag is very leg-weary!'

Little Toomai lay back and slept all through the long

afternoon and into the twilight, and while he slept Petersen Sahib and Machua Appa followed the track of the two elephants for fifteen miles across the hills. Petersen Sahib had spent eighteen years in catching elephants, and he had only once before found such a dance-place. Machua Appa had no need to look twice at the clearing to see what had been done there, or to scratch with his toe in the packed, rammed earth.

'The child speaks truth,' said he. 'All this was done last night, and I have counted seventy tracks crossing the river. See, Sahib, where Pudmini's leg-iron cut the bark off that tree! Yes; she was there, too.'

They looked at each other, and up and down, and they wondered; for the ways of elephants are beyond the wit of any man, black or white, to fathom.

'Forty years and five,' said Machua Appa, 'have I followed my lord the elephant, but never have I heard that any child of man had seen what this child has seen. By all the Gods of the Hills, it is—what can we say?' and he shook his head.

When they got back to camp it was time for the evening meal. Petersen Sahib ate alone in his tent, but he gave orders that the camp should have two sheep and some fowls, as well as a double ration of flour and rice and salt, for he knew that there would be a feast.

Big Toomai had come up hot-foot from the camp in the plains to search for his son and his elephant, and now that he had found them he looked at them as though he were afraid of them both. And there was a feast by the blazing camp-fires in front of the lines of picketed elephants, and Little Toomai was the hero of it all; and the big brown elephant-catchers, the trackers and drivers and ropers, and the men who know all the secrets of breaking the wildest elephants, passed him from one to the other, and they marked his forehead with blood from the breast of a newly killed jungle-cock, to show that he was a forester, initiated and free of all the jungles.

And at last, when the flames died down, and the red light of the logs made the elephants look as though they had been dipped in blood too, Machua Appa, the head of all the drivers of all the Keddahs—Machua Appa, Petersen Sahib's other self, who had never seen a made road in forty years: Machua Appa, who was so great that he had no other name than Machua Appa—leaped to his feet, with Little Toomai held high in the air above his head, and shouted: 'Listen, my brothers. Listen, too, you my lords in the lines there, for I, Machua Appa, am speaking! This little one shall no more be called Little Toomai, but Toomai of the Elephants, as his great-grandfather was called before him. What never man has seen he has seen through the long night, and the favour of the elephant-folk and of the gods of the jungles is with him. He shall become a great tracker; he shall become greater than I, even I—Machua Appa! He shall follow the new trail, and the stale trail, and the mixed trail, with a clear eye! He shall take no harm in the Keddah when he runs under their bellies to rope the wild tuskers; and if he slips before the feet of the charging bull-elephant, that bull-elephant shall know who he is and shall not crush him. Aihai! my lords in the chains,'—he whirled up the line of pickets—'here is the little one that has seen your dances in your hidden places—the sight that never man saw! Give him honour, my lords! *Salaam karo*, my children! Make your salute to Toomai of the Elephants! Gunga Pershad, ahaa! Hira Guj, Birchi Guj, Kuttar Guj, ahaa! Pudmini,—thou hast seen him at the dance, and thou too, Kala Nag, my pearl among elephants!—Ahaa! Together! To Toomai of the Elephants. Barmo!'

And at that last wild yell the whole line flung up their trunks till the tips touched their foreheads, and broke out into the full salute, the crashing trumpet-peal that only the Viceroy of India hears—the Salaam-ut of the Keddah.

But it was all for the sake of Little Toomai, who had seen what never man had seen before—the dance of the elephants at night and alone in the heart of the Garo hills!

From *The Jungle Book*

THE TIGER IN THE TUNNEL

Ruskin Bond

Tembu, the boy, opened his eyes in the dark and wondered if his father was ready to leave the hut on his nightly errand. There was no moon that night, and the deathly stillness of the surrounding jungle was broken only occasionally by the shrill cry of a cicada. Sometimes from far off came the hollow hammering of a woodpecker carried along on the faint breeze. Or the grunt of a wild boar could be heard as he dug up a favourite root. But these sounds were rare and the silence of the forest always returned to swallow them up.

Baldeo, the watchman, was awake. He stretched himself, slowly unwinding the heavy shawl that covered him like a shroud. It was close to midnight and the chill air made him shiver. The station, a small shack backed by heavy jungle, was a station in name only; for trains only stopped there, if at all, for a few seconds before entering the deep cutting that led to the tunnel. Most trains merely slowed down before taking the sharp curve before the cutting.

Baldeo was responsible for signalling whether or not the tunnel was clear of obstruction, and his hand-worked signal stood before the entrance. At night it was his duty to see that the lamp was burning, and that the overland mail passed through safely.

'Shall I come too, Father?' asked Tembu sleepily, still lying huddled in a corner of the hut.

'No, it is cold tonight. Do not get up.'

Tembu, who was twelve, did not always sleep with his father at the station, for he had also to help in the home, where his mother and younger sister were usually alone. They lived in a small tribal village on the outskirts of the forest, about three miles from the station. Their small rice fields did not provide them with more than a bare living and Baldeo considered himself lucky to have got the job of khalasi at this small wayside signal stop.

Still drowsy, Baldeo groped for his lamp in the darkness, then fumbled about in search of matches. When he had produced a light, he left the hut, closed the door behind him, and set off along the permanent way. Tembu had fallen asleep again.

Baldeo wondered whether the lamp on the signal post was still alight. Gathering his shawl closer about him, he stumbled on, sometimes along the rails, sometimes along the ballast. He longed to get back to his warm corner in the hut.

The eeriness of the place was increased by the neighbouring hills which overhung the main line threateningly. On entering the cutting with its sheer rock walls towering high above the rails, Baldeo could not help thinking about the wild animals he might encounter. He had heard many tales of the famous tunnel tiger, a man-eater, who was supposed to frequent this spot; but he hardly believed these stories for, since his arrival at this place a month ago, he had not seen or even heard a tiger.

There had, of course, been panthers, and only a few days

ago the villagers had killed one with their spears and axes. Baldeo had occasionally heard the sawing of a panther calling to its mate, but they had not come near the tunnel or shed.

Baldeo walked confidently for, being tribal himself, he was used to the jungle and its ways. Like his forefathers, he carried a small axe; fragile to look at, but deadly when in use. With it, in three or four swift strokes, he could cut down a tree as neatly as if it had been sawn; and he prided himself in his skill in wielding it against wild animals. He had killed a young boar with it once, and the family had feasted on the flesh for three days. The axe head of pure steel, thin but ringing true like a bell, had been made by his father over a charcoal fire. This axe was part of himself and wherever he went, be it to the local market seven miles away, or to a tribal dance, the axe was always in his hand. Occasionally an official who had come to the station had offered him good money for the weapons; but Baldeo had no intention of parting with it.

The cutting curved sharply, and in the darkness the black entrance to the tunnel loomed up menacingly. The signal light was out. Baldeo set to work to haul the lamp down by its chain. If the oil had finished, he would have to return to the hut for more. The mail train was due in five minutes.

Once more he fumbled for his matches. Then suddenly he stood still and listened. The frightened cry of a barking deer, followed by a crashing sound in the undergrowth, made Baldeo hurry. There was still a little oil in the lamp, and after an instant's hesitation he lit the lamp again and hoisted it back into position. Having done this, he walked quickly down the tunnel, swinging his own lamp, so that the shadows leapt up and down the soot-stained walls, and having made sure that the line was clear, he returned to the entrance and sat down to wait for the mail train.

The train was late. Sitting huddled up, almost dozing, he soon forgot his surroundings and began to nod.

Back in the hut, the trembling of the ground told of the approach of the train, and a low, distant rumble woke the boy, who sat up, rubbing the sleep from his eyes.

'Father, it's time to light the lamp,' he mumbled, and then, realizing that his father had been gone some time, he lay down again, but he was wide awake now, waiting for the train to pass, waiting for his father's returning footsteps.

A low grunt resounded from the top of the cutting. In a second Baldeo was awake, all his senses alert. Only a tiger could emit such a sound.

There was no shelter for Baldeo, but he grasped his axe firmly and tensed his body, trying to make out the direction from which the animal was approaching. For some time there was only silence, even the usual jungle noises seemed to have ceased altogether. Then a thump and the rattle of small stones announced that the tiger had sprung into the cutting.

Baldeo, listening as he had never listened before, wondered if it was making for the tunnel or the opposite direction— the direction of the hut, in which Tembu would be lying unprotected. He did not have to wonder for long. Before a minute had passed he made out the huge body of the tiger trotting steadily towards him. Its eyes shone a brilliant green in the light from the signal lamp. Flight was useless, for in the dark the tiger would be more sure-footed than Baldeo and would soon be upon him from behind. Baideo stood with his back to the signal post, motionless, staring at the great brute moving rapidly towards him. The tiger, used to the ways of men, for it had been preying on them for years, came on fearlessly, and with a quick turn and a snarl struck out with its right paw, expecting to bowl over this puny man who dared stand in the way.

Baldeo, however, was ready. With a marvelously agile leap he avoided the paw and brought his axe down on the animal's shoulder. The tiger gave a roar and attempted to close in. Again Baldeo drove his axe with true aim; but, to his horror, the beast swerved, and the axe caught the tiger on the shoulder, almost severing the leg. To make matters worse, the axe remained stuck in the bone, and Baldeo was left without a weapon.

The tiger, roaring with pain, now sprang upon Baldeo, bringing him down and then tearing at his broken body. It was all over in a few minutes. Baldeo was conscious only of a searing pain down his back, and then there was blackness and the night closed in on him forever.

The tiger drew off and sat down licking his wounded leg, roaring every now and then with agony. He did not notice the faint rumble that shook the earth, followed by the distant puffing of an engine steadily climbing. The overland mail was approaching. Through the trees beyond the cutting, as the train advanced, the glow of the furnace could be seen, and showers of sparks fell like Diwali lights over the forest.

As the train entered the cutting, the engine whistled once, loud and piercingly. The tiger raised his head, then slowly got to his feet. He found himself trapped like the man. Flight along the cutting was impossible. He entered the tunnel, running as fast as his wounded leg would carry him. And then, with a roar and a shower of sparks, the train entered the yawning tunnel. The noise in the confined space was deafening but, when the train came out into the open, on the other side, silence returned once more to the forest and the tunnel.

At the next station the driver slowed down and stopped his

train to water the engine. He got down to stretch his legs and decided to examine the headlamps. He received the surprise of his life; for, just above the cowcatcher lay the major portion of the tiger, cut in half by the engine.

There was considerable excitement and conjecture at the station, but back at the cutting there was no sound except for the sobs of the boy as he sat beside the body of his father. He sat there a long time, unafraid of the darkness, guarding the body from jackals and hyenas, until the first faint light of dawn brought with it the arrival of the relief watchman.

Tembu and his sister and mother were plunged in grief for two whole days; but life had to go on, and a living had to be made, and all the responsibility now fell on Tembu. Three nights later, he was at the cutting, lighting the signal lamp for the overland mail.

He sat down in the darkness to wait for the train, and sang softly to himself. There was nothing to be afraid of—his father had killed the tiger, the forest gods were pleased; and besides, he had the axe with him, his father's axe, and he knew how to use it.

RIKKI-TIKKI-TAVI

Rudyard Kipling

>At the hole where he went in
>Red-Eye called to Wrinkle-Skin.
>Hear what little Red-Eye saith:
>'Nag, come up and dance with death!'
>
>Eye to eye and head to head,
>   (Keep the measure, Nag.)
>This shall end when one is dead;
>   (At thy pleasure, Nag.)
>Turn for turn and twist for twist—
>   (Run and hide thee, Nag.)
>Hah! The hooded Death has missed!
>   (Woe betide thee, Nag!)

This is the story of the great war that Rikki-tikki-tavi fought single-handed, through the bathrooms of the big bungalow in Segowlee cantonment. Darzee, the tailorbird, helped him, and Chuchundra, the musk-rat, who never comes out into the middle of the floor, but always creeps round by the wall, gave him advice; but Rikki-tikki did the real fighting.

He was a mongoose, rather like a little cat in his fur and his tail, but quite like a weasel in his head and his habits. His eyes and the end of his restless nose were pink. He could scratch himself anywhere he pleased with any leg, front or back, that he chose to use. He could fluff up his tail till it looked like a bottle brush, and his war cry as he scuttled through the long grass was: '*Rikk-tikk-tikki-tikki-tchk!*'

One day, a high summer flood washed him out of the burrow where he lived with his father and mother, and carried him, kicking and clucking, down a roadside ditch. He found a little wisp of grass floating there, and clung to it till he lost his senses. When he revived, he was lying in the hot sun on the middle of a garden path, very draggled indeed, and a small boy was saying, 'Here's a dead mongoose. Let's have a funeral.'

'No,' said his mother, 'let's take him in and dry him. Perhaps he isn't really dead.'

They took him into the house, and a big man picked him up between his finger and thumb and said he was not dead but half-choked. So they wrapped him in cotton wool, and warmed him over a little fire, and he opened his eyes and sneezed.

'Now,' said the big man (he was an Englishman who had just moved into the bungalow), 'don't frighten him, and we'll see what he'll do.'

It is the hardest thing in the world to frighten a mongoose, because he is eaten up from nose to tail with curiosity. The motto of all the mongoose family is, 'Run and find out;' and Rikki-tikki was a true mongoose. He looked at the cotton wool, decided that it was not good to eat, ran all round the table, sat up and put his fur in order, scratched himself, and jumped on the small boy's shoulder.

'Don't be frightened, Teddy,' said his father. 'That's his way of making friends.'

'Ouch! He's tickling under my chin,' said Teddy.

Rikki-tikki looked down between the boy's collar and neck, snuffed at his ear, and climbed down to the floor, where he sat rubbing his nose.

'Good gracious,' said Teddy's mother, 'and that's a wild creature! I suppose he's so tame because we've been kind to him.'

'All mongooses are like that,' said her husband. 'If Teddy doesn't pick him up by the tail, or try to put him in a cage, he'll run in and out of the house all day long. Let's give him something to eat.'

They gave him a little piece of raw meat. Rikki-tikki liked it immensely, and when it was finished he went out into the verandah and sat in the sunshine and fluffed up his fur to make it dry to the roots. Then he felt better.

'There are more things to find out about in this house,' he said to himself, 'than all my family could find out in all their lives. I shall certainly stay and find out.'

He spent all that day roaming over the house. He nearly drowned himself in the bathtubs, put his nose into the ink on a writing table, and burned it on the end of the big man's cigar, for he climbed up in the big man's lap to see how writing was done. At nightfall he ran into Teddy's nursery to watch how kerosene lamps were lighted, and when Teddy went to bed Rikki-tikki climbed up too. But he was a restless companion, because he had to get up and attend to every noise all through the night, and find out what made it. Teddy's mother and father came in, the last thing, to look at their boy, and Rikki-tikki was awake on the pillow. 'I don't like that,' said Teddy's mother. 'He may bite the child.' 'He'll do no such thing,' said the father.

'Teddy's safer with that little beast than if he had a bloodhound to watch him. If a snake came into the nursery now—'

But Teddy's mother wouldn't think of anything so awful.

Early in the morning Rikki-tikki came to breakfast in the verandah riding on Teddy's shoulder, and they gave him banana and some boiled egg. He sat on all their laps one after the other, because every well-brought-up mongoose always hopes to be a house mongoose some day and have rooms to run about in; and Rikki-tikki's mother (she used to live in the general's house at Segowlee) had carefully told Rikki what to do if ever he came across white men.

Then Rikki-tikki went out into the garden to see what was to be seen. It was a large garden, only half cultivated, with bushes, as big as summerhouses, of Marshal Niel roses, lime and orange trees, clumps of bamboos, and thickets of high grass. Rikki-tikki licked his lips. 'This is a splendid hunting-ground,' he said, and his tail grew bottle-brushy at the thought of it, and he scuttled up and down the garden, snuffing here and there till he heard very sorrowful voices in a thornbush.

It was Darzee, the tailorbird, and his wife. They had made a beautiful nest by pulling two big leaves together and stitching them up the edges with fibers, and had filled the hollow with cotton and downy fluff. The nest swayed to and fro, as they sat on the rim and cried.

'What is the matter?' asked Rikki-tikki.

'We are very miserable,' said Darzee. 'One of our babies fell out of the nest yesterday and Nag ate him.'

'H'm!' said Rikki-tikki, 'that is very sad—but I am a stranger here. Who is Nag?'

Darzee and his wife only cowered down in the nest without answering, for from the thick grass at the foot of the bush there came a low hiss—a horrid cold sound that made Rikki-tikki jump back two clear feet. Then inch by inch out of the grass rose up the head and spread hood of Nag, the big black cobra, and he was five feet long from tongue to tail. When he had lifted one-third of himself clear of the ground, he stayed balancing to and fro exactly as a dandelion tuft balances in the wind, and he looked at Rikki-tikki with the wicked snake's eyes that never change their expression, whatever the snake may be thinking of.

'Who is Nag?' said he. '*I* am Nag. The great God Brahm put his mark upon all our people, when the first cobra spread his hood to keep the sun off Brahm as he slept. Look, and be afraid!'

He spread out his hood more than ever, and Rikki-tikki saw the spectacle-mark on the back of it that looks exactly like the eye part of a hook-and-eye fastening. He was afraid for a minute; but it is impossible for a mongoose to stay frightened for any length of time, and though Rikki-tikki had never met a live cobra before, his mother had fed him on dead ones, and he knew that all a grown mongoose's business in life was to fight and eat snakes. Nag knew that too and, at the bottom of his cold heart, he was afraid.

'Well,' said Rikki-tikki, and his tail began to fluff up again, 'marks or no marks, do you think it is right for you to eat fledglings out of a nest?'

Nag was thinking to himself, and watching the least little movement in the grass behind Rikki-tikki. He knew that mongooses in the garden meant death sooner or later for him and his family, but he wanted to get Rikki-tikki off his guard. So he dropped his head a little, and put it on one side.

'Let us talk,' he said. 'You eat eggs. Why should not I eat birds?'

'Behind you! Look behind you!' sang Darzee.

Rikki-tikki knew better than to waste time in staring. He jumped up in the air as high as he could go, and just under him whizzed by the head of Nagaina, Nag's wicked wife. She had crept up behind him as he was talking, to make an end of him. He heard her savage hiss as the stroke missed. He came down almost across her back, and if he had been an old mongoose he would have known that then was the time to break her back with one bite; but he was afraid of the terrible lashing return stroke of the cobra. He bit, indeed, but did not bite long enough, and he jumped clear of the whisking tail, leaving Nagaina torn and angry.

'Wicked, wicked Darzee!' said Nag, lashing up as high as he could reach toward the nest in the thornbush. But Darzee had built it out of reach of snakes, and it only swayed to and fro.

Rikki-tikki felt his eyes growing red and hot (when a mongoose's eyes grow red, he is angry), and he sat back on his tail and hind legs like a little kangaroo, and looked all round him, and chattered with rage. But Nag and Nagaina had disappeared into the grass. When a snake misses its stroke, it never says anything or gives any sign of what it means to do next. Rikki-tikki did not care to follow them, for he did not feel sure that he could manage two snakes at once. So, he trotted off to the gravel path near the house, and sat down to think. It was a serious matter for him.

If you read the old books of natural history, you will find they say that when the mongoose fights the snake and happens to get bitten, he runs off and eats some herb that cures him. That is not true. The victory is only a matter of quickness of eye and quickness of foot—snake's blow against mongoose's jump—and as no eye can follow the motion of a snake's head when it strikes, this makes things much more wonderful than any magic herb. Rikki-tikki knew he was a young mongoose, and it made him all the more pleased to think that he had managed to escape a blow from behind. It gave him confidence in himself, and when Teddy came running down the path, Rikki-tikki was ready to be petted.

But just as Teddy was stooping, something wriggled a little in the dust, and a tiny voice said: 'Be careful. I am Death!' It was Karait, the dusty brown snakeling that lies for choice on the dusty earth; and his bite is as dangerous as the cobra's. But he is so small that nobody thinks of him, and so he does the more harm to people.

Rikki-tikki's eyes grew red again, and he danced up to Karait with the peculiar rocking, swaying motion that he had inherited from his family. It looks very funny, but it is so perfectly balanced a gait that you can fly off from it at any angle you please, and in dealing with snakes this is an advantage. If Rikki-tikki had only known, he was doing a much more dangerous thing than fighting Nag, for Karait is so small, and can turn so quickly, that unless Rikki bit him close to the back of the head, he would get the return stroke in his eye or his lip. But Rikki did not know. His eyes were all red, and he rocked back and forth, looking for a good place to hold. Karait struck out. Rikki jumped sideways and tried to run in, but the wicked little dusty grey head lashed within a fraction of his shoulder, and he had to jump over the body, and the head followed his heels close.

Teddy shouted to the house: 'Oh, look here! Our mongoose is killing a snake.' And Rikki-tikki heard a scream from Teddy's mother. His father ran out with a stick, but by the time he came up, Karait had lunged out once too far, and Rikki-tikki had sprung, jumped on the snake's back, dropped his head far between his forelegs, bitten as high up the back as he could get hold, and rolled away. That bite paralyzed Karait, and Rikki-tikki was just going to eat him up from the tail, after the custom of his family at dinner, when he remembered that a full meal makes a slow mongoose, and if he wanted all his strength and quickness ready, he must keep himself thin.

He went away for a dust bath under the castor-oil bushes, while Teddy's father beat the dead Karait. 'What is the use of that?' thought Rikki-tikki. 'I have settled it all;' and then Teddy's mother picked him up from the dust and hugged him, crying that he had saved Teddy from death, and Teddy's father said that he was a providence, and Teddy looked on with big scared eyes. Rikki-tikki was rather amused at all the fuss, which, of course, he did not understand. Teddy's mother might just as well have petted Teddy for playing in the dust. Rikki was thoroughly enjoying himself.

That night at dinner, walking to and fro among the wine-glasses on the table, he might have stuffed himself three times over with nice things. But he remembered Nag and Nagaina, and though it was very pleasant to be patted and petted by Teddy's mother, and to sit on Teddy's shoulder, his eyes would get red from time to time, and he would go off into his long war cry of *'Rikk-tikk-tikki-tikki-tchk!'*

Teddy carried him off to bed, and insisted on Rikki-tikki sleeping under his chin. Rikki-tikki was too well-bred to bite or scratch, but as soon as Teddy was asleep he went off for his nightly walk round the house, and in the dark he ran up against Chuchundra, the musk-rat, creeping around by the wall. Chuchundra is a broken-hearted little beast. He whimpers and cheeps all the night, trying to make up his mind to run into the middle of the room. But he never gets there.

'Don't kill me,' said Chuchundra, almost weeping. 'Rikki-tikki, don't kill me!'

'Do you think a snake-killer kills musk-rats?' said Rikki-tikki scornfully.

'Those who kill snakes get killed by snakes,' said Chuchundra, more sorrowfully than ever. 'And how am I to be sure that Nag won't mistake me for you some dark night?'

'There's not the least danger,' said Rikki-tikki. 'But Nag is in the garden, and I know you don't go there.'

'My cousin Chua, the rat, told me—' said Chuchundra, and then he stopped.

'Told you what?'

'H'sh! Nag is everywhere, Rikki-tikki. You should have talked to Chua in the garden.'

'I didn't—so you must tell me. Quick, Chuchundra, or I'll bite you!'

Chuchundra sat down and cried till the tears rolled off his whiskers. 'I am a very poor man,' he sobbed. 'I never had spirit enough to run out into the middle of the room. H'sh! I mustn't tell you anything. Can't you *hear*, Rikki-tikki?'

Rikki-tikki listened. The house was as still as still, but he thought he could just catch the faintest scratch-scratch in the world—a noise as faint as that of a wasp walking on a window-pane—the dry scratch of a snake's scales on brickwork.

'That's Nag or Nagaina,' he said to himself, 'and he is crawling into the bathroom sluice. You're right, Chuchundra; I should have talked to Chua.'

He stole off to Teddy's bathroom, but there was nothing there, and then to Teddy's mother's bathroom. At the bottom of the smooth plaster wall there was a brick pulled out to make a sluice for the bath water, and as Rikki-tikki stole in by the masonry curb where the bath is put, he heard Nag and Nagaina whispering together outside in the moonlight.

'When the house is emptied of people,' said Nagaina to her husband, '*he* will have to go away, and then the garden will be our own again. Go in quietly, and remember that the big man who killed Karait is the first one to bite. Then come out and tell me, and we will hunt for Rikki-tikki together.'

'But are you sure that there is anything to be gained by killing the people?' said Nag.

'Everything. When there were no people in the bungalow, did we have any mongoose in the garden? So long as the bungalow is empty, we are king and queen of the garden; and remember that as soon as our eggs in the melon bed hatch (as they may tomorrow), our children will need room and quiet.'

'I had not thought of that,' said Nag. 'I will go, but there is no need that we should hunt for Rikki-tikki afterward. I will kill the big man and his wife, and the child if I can, and come away quietly. Then the bungalow will be empty, and Rikki-tikki will go.'

Rikki-tikki tingled all over with rage and hatred at this, and then Nag's head came through the sluice, and his five feet of cold body followed it. Angry as he was, Rikki-tikki was very frightened as he saw the size of the big cobra. Nag coiled himself up, raised his head, and looked into the bathroom in the dark, and Rikki could see his eyes glitter.

'Now, if I kill him here, Nagaina will know; and if I fight him on the open floor, the odds are in his favour. What am I to do?' said Rikki-tikki-tavi.

Nag waved to and fro, and then Rikki-tikki heard him drinking from the biggest water-jar that was used to fill the bath. 'That is good,' said the snake. 'Now, when Karait was killed, the big man had a stick. He may have that stick still, but when he comes in to bathe in the morning he will not have a stick. I shall wait here till he comes. Nagaina—do you hear me?—I shall wait here in the cool till daytime.'

There was no answer from outside, so Rikki-tikki knew Nagaina had gone away. Nag coiled himself down, coil by coil, round the bulge at the bottom of the water jar, and Rikki-tikki stayed still as death. After an hour he began to move, muscle by muscle, toward the jar. Nag was asleep, and Rikki-tikki looked at his big back, wondering which would be the best place for a good hold. 'If I don't break his back at the first jump,' said Rikki, 'he can still fight. And if he fights—O Rikki!' He looked at the thickness of the neck below the hood, but that was too much for him; and a bite near the tail would only make Nag savage.

'It must be the head,' he said at last; 'the head above the hood. And, when I am once there, I must not let go.'

Then he jumped. The head was lying a little clear of the water jar, under the curve of it; and, as his teeth met, Rikki braced his back against the bulge of the red earthenware to hold down the head. This gave him just one second's purchase, and he made the most of it. Then he was battered to and fro as a rat is shaken by a dog—to and fro on the floor, up and down, and around in great circles, but his eyes were red and he held on as the body cart-whipped over the floor, upsetting the tin dipper and the soap dish and the flesh brush, and banged against the tin side of the bath. As he held he closed his jaws tighter and tighter, for he made sure he would be banged to death, and, for the honour of his family, he preferred to be found with his teeth locked. He was dizzy, aching, and felt shaken to pieces when something went off like a thunderclap just behind him. A hot wind knocked him senseless and red fire singed his fur.

The big man had been wakened by the noise, and had fired both barrels of a shotgun into Nag just behind the hood.

Rikki-tikki held on with his eyes shut, for now he was quite sure he was dead. But the head did not move, and the big man picked him up and said, 'It's the mongoose again, Alice. The little chap has saved *our* lives now.' Then Teddy's mother came in with a very white face, and saw what was left of Nag, and Rikki-tikki dragged himself to Teddy's bedroom and spent half the rest of the night shaking himself tenderly to find out whether he really was broken into forty pieces, as he fancied.

When morning came he was very stiff, but well pleased with his doings. 'Now I have Nagaina to settle with, and she will be worse than five Nags, and there's no knowing when the eggs she spoke of will hatch. Goodness! I must go and see Darzee,' he said.

Without waiting for breakfast, Rikki-tikki ran to the thornbush where Darzee was singing a song of triumph at the top of his voice. The news of Nag's death was all over the garden, for the sweeper had thrown the body on the rubbish-heap.

'Oh, you stupid tuft of feathers!' said Rikki-tikki angrily. 'Is this the time to sing?'

'Nag is dead—is dead—is dead!' sang Darzee. 'The valiant Rikki-tikki caught him by the head and held fast. The big man brought the bang-stick, and Nag fell in two pieces! He will never eat my babies again.'

'All that's true enough. But where's Nagaina?' said Rikki-tikki, looking carefully round him.

'Nagaina came to the bathroom sluice and called for Nag,' Darzee went on, 'and Nag came out on the end of a stick—the sweeper picked him up on the end of a stick and threw him upon the rubbish heap. Let us sing about the great, the red-eyed Rikki-tikki!' And Darzee filled his throat and sang.

'If I could get up to your nest, I'd roll your babies out!' said Rikki-tikki. 'You don't know when to do the right thing at the right time. You're safe enough in your nest there, but it's war for me down here. Stop singing a minute, Darzee.'

'For the great, the beautiful Rikki-tikki's sake I will stop,' said Darzee. 'What is it, O Killer of the terrible Nag?'

'Where is Nagaina, for the third time?'

'On the rubbish heap by the stables, mourning for Nag. Great is Rikki-tikki with the white teeth.'

'Bother my white teeth! Have you ever heard where she keeps her eggs?'

'In the melon-bed, on the end nearest the wall, where the sun strikes nearly all day. She hid them there weeks ago.'

'And you never thought it worth while to tell me? The end nearest the wall, you said?'

'Rikki-tikki, you are not going to eat her eggs?'

'Not eat exactly; no. Darzee, if you have a grain of sense you will fly off to the stables and pretend that your wing is broken, and let Nagaina chase you away to this bush. I must get to the melon-bed, and if I went there now she'd see me.'

Darzee was a feather-brained little fellow who could never hold more than one idea at a time in his head. And just because he knew that Nagaina's children were born in eggs like his own, he didn't think at first that it was fair to kill them. But his wife was a sensible bird, and she knew that cobra's eggs meant young cobras later on. So she flew off from the nest, and left Darzee to keep the babies warm, and continue his song about the death of Nag. Darzee was very like a man in some ways.

She fluttered in front of Nagaina by the rubbish heap and

cried out, 'Oh, my wing is broken! The boy in the house threw a stone at me and broke it.' Then she fluttered more desperately than ever.

Nagaina lifted up her head and hissed, 'You warned Rikki-tikki when I would have killed him. Indeed and truly, you've chosen a bad place to be lame in.' And she moved toward Darzee's wife, slipping along over the dust.

'The boy broke it with a stone!' shrieked Darzee's wife.

'Well! It may be some consolation to you when you're dead to know that I shall settle accounts with the boy. My husband lies on the rubbish heap this morning, but before night the boy in the house will lie very still. What is the use of running away? I am sure to catch you. Little fool, look at me!'

Darzee's wife knew better than to do *that*, for a bird who looks at a snake's eyes gets so frightened that she cannot move. Darzee's wife fluttered on, piping sorrowfully, and never leaving the ground, and Nagaina quickened her pace.

Rikki-tikki heard them going up the path from the stables, and he raced for the end of the melon patch near the wall. There, in the warm litter above the melons, very cunningly hidden, he found twenty-five eggs, about the size of a bantam's eggs, but with whitish skin instead of shell.

'I was not a day too soon,' he said, for he could see the baby cobras curled up inside the skin, and he knew that the minute they were hatched they could each kill a man or a mongoose. He bit off the tops of the eggs as fast as he could, taking care to crush the young cobras, and turned over the litter from time to time to see whether he had missed any. At last there were only three eggs left, and Rikki-tikki began to chuckle to himself, when he heard Darzee's wife screaming:

'Rikki-tikki, I led Nagaina toward the house, and she has

gone into the verandah, and—oh, come quickly—she means killing!'

Rikki-tikki smashed two eggs, and tumbled backward down the melon-bed with the third egg in his mouth, and scuttled to the verandah as hard as he could put foot to the ground. Teddy and his mother and father were there at early breakfast, but Rikki-tikki saw that they were not eating anything. They sat stone-still, and their faces were white. Nagaina was coiled up on the matting by Teddy's chair, within easy striking distance of Teddy's bare leg, and she was swaying to and fro, singing a song of triumph.

'Son of the big man that killed Nag,' she hissed, 'stay still. I am not ready yet. Wait a little. Keep very still, all you three! If you move I strike, and if you do not move I strike. Oh, foolish people, who killed my Nag!'

Teddy's eyes were fixed on his father, and all his father could do was to whisper, 'Sit still, Teddy. You mustn't move. Teddy, keep still.'

Then Rikki-tikki came up and cried, 'Turn round, Nagaina. Turn and fight!'

'All in good time,' said she, without moving her eyes. 'I will settle my account with *you* presently. Look at your friends, Rikki-tikki. They are still and white. They are afraid. They dare not move, and if you come a step nearer I strike.'

'Look at your eggs,' said Rikki-tikki, 'in the melon bed near the wall. Go and look, Nagaina!'

The big snake turned half around, and saw the egg on the verandah. 'Ah-h! Give it to me,' she said.

Rikki-tikki put his paws one on each side of the egg, and his eyes were blood-red. 'What price for a snake's egg? For a young cobra? For a young king cobra? For the last—the very last of the brood? The ants are eating all the others down by the melon bed.'

Nagaina spun clear round, forgetting everything for the sake of the one egg. Rikki-tikki saw Teddy's father shoot out a big hand, catch Teddy by the shoulder, and drag him across the little table with the teacups, safe and out of reach of Nagaina.

'Tricked! Tricked! Tricked! *Rikk-tck-tck!*' chuckled Rikki-tikki. 'The boy is safe, and it was I—I—I that caught Nag by the hood last night in the bathroom.' Then he began to jump up and down, all four feet together, his head close to the floor. 'He threw me to and fro, but he could not shake me off. He was dead before the big man blew him in two. I did it! *Rikki-tikki-tck-tck!* Come then, Nagaina. Come and fight with me. You shall not be a widow long.'

Nagaina saw that she had lost her chance of killing Teddy, and the egg lay between Rikki-tikki's paws. 'Give me the egg, Rikki-tikki. Give me the last of my eggs, and I will go away and never come back,' she said, lowering her hood.

'Yes, you will go away, and you will never come back. For you will go to the rubbish heap with Nag. Fight, widow! The big man has gone for his gun! Fight!'

Rikki-tikki was bounding all round Nagaina, keeping just out of reach of her stroke, his little eyes like hot coals. Nagaina gathered herself together and flung out at him. Rikki-tikki jumped up and backward. Again and again and again she struck, and each time her head came with a whack on the matting of the verandah and she gathered herself together like a watch spring. Then Rikki-tikki danced in a circle to get behind her, and Nagaina spun round to keep her head to his head, so that the rustle of her tail on the matting sounded like dry leaves blown along by the wind.

He had forgotten the egg. It still lay on the verandah, and Nagaina came nearer and nearer to it, till at last, while Rikki-tikki was drawing breath, she caught it in her mouth, turned to the verandah steps, and flew like an arrow down the path, with Rikki-tikki behind her. When the cobra runs for her life, she goes like a whiplash flicked across a horse's neck.

Rikki-tikki knew that he must catch her, or all the trouble would begin again. She headed straight for the long grass by the thornbush, and as he was running Rikki-tikki heard Darzee still singing his foolish little song of triumph. But Darzee's wife was wiser. She flew off her nest as Nagaina came along, and flapped her wings about Nagaina's head. If Darzee had helped they might have turned her, but Nagaina only lowered her hood and went on. Still, the instant's delay brought Rikki-tikki up to her, and as she plunged into the rat-hole where she and Nag used to live, his little white teeth were clenched on her tail, and he went down with her—and very few mongooses, however wise and old they may be, care to follow a cobra into its hole. It was dark in the hole; and Rikki-tikki never knew when it might open out and give Nagaina room to turn and strike at him. He held on savagely, and stuck out his feet to act as brakes on the dark slope of the hot, moist earth.

Then the grass by the mouth of the hole stopped waving, and Darzee said, 'It is all over with Rikki-tikki! We must sing his death song. Valiant Rikki-tikki is dead! For Nagaina will surely kill him underground.'

So he sang a very mournful song that he made up on the spur of the minute, and just as he got to the most touching part, the grass quivered again, and Rikki-tikki, covered with dirt, dragged himself out of the hole leg by leg, licking his whiskers. Darzee stopped with a little shout. Rikki-tikki shook some of the dust out of his fur and sneezed. 'It is all over,' he said. 'The widow will never come out again.' And the red ants that live between the grass stems heard him, and began to troop down one after another to see if he had spoken the truth.

Rikki-tikki curled himself up in the grass and slept where he was—slept and slept till it was late in the afternoon, for he had done a hard day's work.

'Now,' he said, when he awoke, 'I will go back to the house. Tell the Coppersmith, Darzee, and he will tell the garden that Nagaina is dead.'

The Coppersmith is a bird who makes a noise exactly like the beating of a little hammer on a copper pot; and the reason he is always making it is because he is the town crier to every Indian garden, and tells all the news to everybody who cares to listen. As Rikki-tikki went up the path, he heard his 'attention' notes like a tiny dinner gong, and then the steady '*Ding-dong-tock!* Nag is dead—dong! Nagaina is dead! *Ding-dong-tock!*' That set all the birds in the garden singing, and the frogs croaking, for Nag and Nagaina used to eat frogs as well as little birds.

When Rikki got to the house, Teddy and Teddy's mother (she looked very white still, for she had been fainting) and Teddy's father came out and almost cried over him; and that night he ate all that was given to him till he could eat no more, and went to bed on Teddy's shoulder, where Teddy's mother saw him when she came to look late at night.

'He saved our lives and Teddy's life,' she said to her husband. 'Just think, he saved all our lives.'

Rikki-tikki woke up with a jump, for the mongooses are light sleepers.

'Oh, it's you,' said he. 'What are you bothering for? All the cobras are dead. And if they weren't, I'm here.'

Rikki-tikki had a right to be proud of himself. But he did not grow too proud, and he kept that garden as a mongoose should keep it, with tooth and jump and spring and bite, till never a cobra dared show its head inside the walls.

◆

Darzee's Chaunt

(Sung in honour of Rikki-tikki-tavi)
Singer and tailor am I—
Doubled the joys that I know—
Proud of my lilt through the sky,
Proud of the house that I sew—

Over and under, so weave I my music—so weave I the house that I sew.

Sing to your fledglings again,
Mother, oh lift up your head!
Evil that plagued us is slain,
Death in the garden lies dead.

Terror that hid in the roses is impotent—flung on the dunghill and dead!

Who has delivered us, who?
Tell me his nest and his name.
Rikki, the valiant, the true,
Tikki, with eyeballs of flame,

Rikk-tikki-tikki, the ivory-fanged, the hunter with eyeballs of flame!

> Give him the Thanks of the Birds,
> Bowing with tail feathers spread!
> Praise him with nightingale-words—
> Nay, I will praise him instead.

Hear! I will sing you the praise of the bottle-tailed Rikki, with eyeballs of red!

(Here Rikki-tikki interrupted, and the rest of the song is lost.)

'SANDY' BERESFORD'S TIGERHUNT

Charles A. Kincaid

Walter Beresford, known to his friends as 'Sandy' because of his reddish-yellow hair, but styled by the Government of Bombay as Mr Walter Trevelyn Beresford, District Superintendent of Police, Dharwar, lay in a long chair on the verandah of the traveller's bungalow at D—, some sixty miles from Dharwar cantonment. In front of him stretched a beautiful little lake, covered here and there with masses of water-lilies; in far corners of it dab-chicks disported themselves, while a bunch or two of teal and an odd 'spotbill' sneaked about, half hidden by the reeds. 'Sandy' had an excellent dinner and felt at peace with the world; moreover, that afternoon he had bagged his seventeenth panther.

The only fly in the ointment of his happiness was that he was alone. It was the first day of the Christmas holidays and he had expected his old friend Ford Halley, the D.S.P. of Belgaum, to be at D— with him. On his arrival that morning at the bungalow, a telegram was handed to him. He opened it and read the following words:

'Very sorry. Detained by a murder case. joining you tomorrow.'

Beresford was thus condemned to spend the next twenty-four hours alone. Happily, Ford Halley would be there for Christmas; so the two friends would eat their Christmas dinner together. On Boxing Day the real business of the camp would begin. They would drive for a man-eating tiger that had been doing a lot of damage over an area of twenty miles round D—. Ford Halley was an old shikari and had at least a dozen tigers to his credit, nor was Sandy Beresford a new hand. He had killed a couple of tigers, two or three bears and sixteen panthers.

During breakfast which Beresford, after a long ride in his car, ate with a first class appetite, his orderly, who also did duty as shikari, came in a state of suppressed excitement. 'Wagh! Sahib! Wagh!' he half-whispered, half-hissed at his master.

Beresford sprang to his feet. 'Patayat Wagh (A Tiger)? or Biblia Wagh (A Panther)?'

'Mothé Thorile nahint. (It is not a tiger). *Biblia Wagh ahe.* (It is a panther)'

Beresford was at first disappointed, but on second thoughts felt a thrill of joy. If he got the panther it would make his seventeenth, only three short of twenty. Twenty panthers were quite a respectable total for a man of only thirteen years' service. He turned to his shikari: 'Well, Dhondu,' he said, 'how far-off' is it?'

'Sahib, it is only the other side of the lake. It killed a young buffalo last night and dragged the kill under a big tree. I have had the kill tied with a rope to the trunk and if the Sahib is ready to come this afternoon about four, I shall have a machan (stand) built and come and fetch the Sahib.'

'Splendid!' said Beresford. 'I shall be ready all right. You had better go back now and rig up the machan, so that all work it requires may be finished before half past three. The panther might wake up then, and it he saw you at work I should get no chance of a shot.'

The shikari salaamed and vanished.

Beresford took his rifle from its case, a .400 Jeffery cordite, that would stop a charging elephant. He glanced down the barrels and satisfied himself that they were beautifully clean; he put the rifle to his shoulder once or twice to see that it came up all right. Next he took out his shotgun which, loaded with SS, he carried always as a second weapon. These preparations finished, he lay in his long chair and smoked and dozed until tea time. A little before four his shikari appeared and the two men went off together.

The shikari had not underestimated the distance. The spot where the kill lay was only half an hour's walk from the bungalow; and when Beresford reached there, he found the man whom the shikari had left in the machan in a great state of excitement. The panther, he said, had come and had looked at the dead buffalo from a distance of fifty yards. Then it had moved away. It was somewhere close by. The Sahib should get into the machan without delay.

Beresford, recognizing the soundness of the advice, climbed as quickly as possible into his hiding place. Ten minutes later he saw dimly the outline of the panther, lying in some bushes fifty yards away. It was too difficult a shot to risk; so he waited. After some five to ten minutes, during which time Beresford's heart thumped so hard that he was afraid the panther would hear it, the brute rose and came towards the kill. It was evidently not very hungry; for instead of beginning at once to tear the flesh, it stood looking at the dead buffalo, as if uncertain with which bit to start its meal. Before it came to any decision, a bullet from Beresford's .400 rendered the question academic. The panther lay dead on its dead victim, of which it would never eat another mouthful.

Beresford came back in excellent spirits, the villagers carrying his seventeenth panther, fastened by its four feet to a long bamboo pole. He tubbed, changed and ate the dinner provided for him with a Spartans appetite, although indeed his cook had served a meal that needed no hunger sauce. Beresford was now reclining in a long chair, as I have said, in the verandah of the bungalow and a golden coloured 'peg' lay within reach of his right hand.

As he lay, he suddenly began to feel creepy. He remembered a story narrated to him, when a boy, of his grandfather General Beresford. The latter, when a young officer, had, shortly after the Mutiny, been posted to Dharwar, and had gone on a shooting trip to the very bungalow where 'Sandy' now resided. He had a horrible experience. Lying in a long chair in the verandah where his grandson now lay, he had gone asleep. By him reclined his friend, Captain Richardson, afterwards General Sir Archibald Richardson. He, too, had dropped off. General Beresford had been awakened by a sharp pain in his left arm. Looking at it, he had seen a tiger standing beside him. It had seized his arm in its mouth and was dragging at it. General Beresford had kept his head and had called to Richardson to fetch a rifle from within and shoot the brute. As the tiger was pulling at his arm, General Beresford had to go with him, for he feared that if he resisted the tiger would kill him outright. He rose and walked alongside the tiger through the compound—a *via dolorosa* as terrible as any in history—hoping always that Richardson would be able to put the rifle together and load it before they reached the compound wall. The idea that Richardson would show the white feather never entered his head; but General Beresford knew that on reaching the compound wall the tiger would take his body into its mouth to leap the wall. He walked step by step, as slowly as he dared. Suddenly he heard a cheery voice and the steps of his friend racing behind him. The tiger seemed utterly contemptuous of the newcomer and stopped near the wall, preparatory to gathering its victims body within its mighty jaws. The moment's pause proved its undoing. Richardson, reaching the tiger's side, knelt down; aiming at its heart, he pulled the trigger. The brute's grip on General Beresford's arm relaxed and it rolled over amid a cloud of smoke. It was stone dead. Richardson had saved his friend's life; but General Beresford's left arm had had to be amputated; and Sandy remembered distinctly the empty sleeve that his grandfather used to wear pinned across his breast.

Sandy looked nervously around and felt very much inclined to run into his bedroom and bolt the door. Then he pulled himself together, smiled at his fears and said half aloud: 'The modern tiger has far too wholesome a respect for the Englishman to behave in that truculent fashion.' To support his statement, he drained the whisky and soda at his side, settled himself once more in his chair and a few minutes later fell fast asleep.

He had a ghastly dream. He dreamt that he had gone to bathe in the lake in front of the bungalow. As he entered the water one of his sepoys ran up and begged him not to, as it was full of 'maghars'. Beresford laughed at the warning and began swimming in the lake. Suddenly an acute pain in his left arm made him realize that the sepoy's warning was one to have been followed. An alligator had seized him by the arm and was trying to pull him under. Struggle as Sandy Beresford might, he was helpless. He cried aloud for help and in doing so woke up, the perspiration streaming down his face.

He gave a sigh of relief and wanted to wipe his face with his handkerchief. He found he could not move his left arm which, moreover, hurt him a good deal. Surprised, he looked and saw that a tiger was standing by his chair and had seized his left arm, just as the other tiger sixty years before had seized his grandfathers By an involuntary trick of memory he called out 'Richardson! Richardson!' Then his blood ran cold as he realized that he was alone in the bungalow. If only Ford Halley had been there; but there was no one. Even the shikari had gone to another village to tie up for the shoot on Boxing Day. There were, it is true, the servants in their quarters; but their doors were certainly barricaded from inside and they would be far too frightened to come outside, even if they knew how to handle a rifle. Sandy Beresford's case was indeed desperate, nevertheless he called out at the top of his voice 'Qui Hail Qui Hail' hoping for some miracle to happen.

No one answered and the tiger, disturbed by the noise, was pulling at Beresford's left arm in a way that took no denial. lust as his grandfather had done, Sandy rose to his feet, and walked alongside the tiger down the verandah steps and across the compound towards the far wall. He continued to call at the top of his voice as he went. He knew that it was wasted breath; still, hope dies hard.

At last, when he was close to the compound wall, he realized that he was a doomed man. Nevertheless, he made a supreme effort to escape. Indeed he actually tore his arm out of the tiger's jaws; but the effort was useless. A stroke of the tiger's paw knocked him senseless to the ground. The tiger's teeth tearing through his heart and lungs effectually prevented his ever recovering consciousness. Taking Beresford's arm again into his mouth, the man-eater skilfully swung the dead man's body across its shoulders and easily clearing the compound wall disappeared into the forest.

Next morning Beresford's cook and butler opened the doors of their quarters and peered outside. Ignorant of the previous night's tragedy, the cook made his master's tea and the butler carried it inside the bungalow. The latter was surprised not to find Beresford in his bedroom and he was still more astonished to notice that his master's bed had not been slept in. He called to the cook and the sepoys. They searched everywhere but in vain. Then the butler saw drops of blood on the floor of the verandah leading into the compound. These they followed until they came to some softer earth where they could make out clearly an Englishmain's footprints and a tiger's pugs. They guessed then that Beresford had fallen a victim to the very man-eater that he had come to kill.

When Ford Halley arrived about eleven, he found his friend's domestic staff in a state of utter perplexity and confusion. The shikari to whom Beresford had related what had happened to his grandfather was loudly proclaiming that the tiger was not an ordinary animal but a demon reincarnation of the beast that Richardson had shot. It was, therefore, useless to hunt it. All that man could do was to flee from the accursed spot as quickly as possible.

Ford Halley brushed aside this fantastic theory and restored some order among the household. He organized a search for Beresford's body and found his half-eaten remains a mile from the bungalow. These he had put into an improvised coffin and sent into Dharwar, where they received a Christian burial. The rest of the holidays he spent hunting the man-eater and was able to put 'paid' to its account on the very last day, namely the second of January. In the meantime, he reported his friends death to the Bombay Government.

When His Excellency learnt the news of the tragedy he wrote a charming letter to Beresford's widowed mother, informing her—which was quite true—how much he regretted her son's death and how greatly he felt the loss of his valuable services.

From his brother officers, Beresford received the epitaph which was usual in such cases:

'Beresford killed by a tiger! By Jove, what bad luck!' After a pause, 'Damn it all! Dharwar is a splendid climate. I wonder whether the government would send me there if I applied for it.'

THE VENGEANCE OF KURNAIL JARN

Jan Kinnsale

Of dubious pedigree but undoubted courage, he was a bull-terrier of some forty muscular pounds. He was known as Kurnail Jarn simply because that was the nearest the 'syces' and 'shikaris' could get to enunciating the name of his original owner, Colonel John Sherer.

Broad-chested, slim-flanked, wedge-headed, cock-eared, he was a menacingly silent animal, and the only things that made him give tongue were new-baked chappatis and the moon coming up over the ricefields.

He was, as are all his breed, a one-man dog, and when, together with the British Raj, Colonel Sherer went home, Kurnail Jarn, left behind through force of many circumstances, mourned his master from the depths of his canine heart.

However, he took his new owner—Donaldson, a mineralogist prospecting for uranium for the Indian Government—on approval, already being acquainted with him by virtue of occasional shikars Donaldson had been on with Colonel Sherer.

The realization that Donaldson was synonymous with the hunting of cheetul and tahr and other exciting things, coupled with the fact that a dog needs somebody on whom to lavish its affection, made Kurnail Jarn in the fulness of time, go out of mourning and transfer his allegiance wholeheartedly to his new master.

In camp somewhere between the Chinkara River and the Gilgit Mountains (that 'between' is a thousand miles, but it is necessary to be vague as the Indian Government still hopes to find uranium there), Donaldson, in the intervals of prospecting, kept his Mannlicher rifle oiled and his eye in practice.

He had hunted most things from muntjac to man-eaters, and now he was in the process of achieving his ambition of shooting a gaur, one of the huge wild cattle of India.

The local ryots, or farmers, had complained to him that an old bull gaur, one of the most dangerous animals in the world, had been playing havoc in their ricefields and begged him to shoot it.

They showed him the waterhole the bull frequented, and Donaldson, accompanied by Kurnail Jarn, duly ensconced himself in a tangle of rocks at the base of a bulbul tree overlooking the waterhole, hoping to catch the gaur in the early morning light.

In that glorious, brittle hour before the sun comes up, when the whole world seems to have been created anew, that exciting hour when the night-hunters steal home to their jungle lairs and the day-hunters are just stirring, Donaldson waited.

Tense, but utterly immobile, knowing that he was only there as a great privilege, Kurnail Jarn sat hidden twenty yards below him.

Away in the jungle a sounder of wild boar grunted on their way home from a good night's foraging; a deer barked...

A jungle-cock began its shrill crowing; a flock of minivets, brilliantly scarlet and yellow, worked through the trees; high overhead a lammergeyer passed on vast wings...

Somewhere a cheetul belled anxiously...

Enured by a hundred shikars, Donaldson waited for the culmination of his vigil, alert to every sound and movement, and praying that the wind would stay where it was.

Nearby, Kurnail Jarn swallowed the saliva in his mouth which he longed to open but dared not.

Suddenly, from the direction of the camp, which lay a mile or two away through the jungle, came a ponderous crashing.

Donaldson frowned in surprise, for he had expected the gaur to appear on his left along the little nullah, or ravine, that led to the water-hole. However, you never could tell and he imperceptibly shifted his grip on the Mannlicher; Kurnail Iarn twitched unbearably.

Through the trees beyond the waterhole a vast mud-grey shape appeared, with great flapping ears and a swaying trunk, while at its side, ludicrous in its small plodding solemnity, marched a miniature replica of the giant: it was Mollie the camp elephant and her three-month-old calf, Dumbell.

Mollie, a maid of all work, as you might say, employed on various heavyweight chores, made a habit of breaking out of her corral to go in search of jungle titbits, which her mahout, Parkash Singh, did not always supply her with, and now she had come to the waterhole to give herself a good plastering of mud before the heat of the day.

Donaldson relaxed and muttered uncomplimentary remarks about elephants in general.

But he did not stir: There might still be a chance of the gaur putting in an appearance.

Meanwhile, Mollie despoiled herself titanically. Dumbell wandered off up the nullah until he was some seventy yards away, contenting himself with sucking up water in his trunk and, like a small boy blowing bubbles, found turgid delight in squirting liquid mud at random.

Distracted by this nonsense, Donaldson did not notice the approach of another visitor to the waterhole. Along the nullah a lithe, striped form had appeared, moving in that typical silken glide which made a wonder of the fact that it was of flesh and bone rather than gorgeous shadow.

The tiger had genuinely come to the waterhole to drink, but seeing the calf-elephant it paused, and other ideas came into its head.

Nine times out of ten the tiger would have left the calf alone; perhaps it had had a poor night's hunting; perhaps it acted on the impulse of the moment. Be that as it may, it crouched and bellied its way towards the innocent Dumbell.

Kurnail Iarn caught sight of the tiger a split second before Donaldson. The tiger gathered itself for the steel-muscled spring. Breaking all the rules, but aware that the elephants were part of the camp and therefore to be protected, Kurnail Jarn bounded down the almost precipitous side of the nullah and hurled himself at the tiger at the very moment the latter sprang at the panic-stricken Dumbell.

Diverted by this flank attack, the tiger hesitated in his leap, clawed superficially at the calf-elephant and turned with a lunging blow on Kurnail Jarn, who was flung a dozen yards away by the vicious sweep.

While the air shrilled with the strident trumpeting of Mollie as she shepherded her squealing, lacerated calf away, Donaldson fired.

The tiger reared up high on its hind legs, clawed the air as if trying to grapple with some unseen foe, gurgled spasmodically, and fell over backwards.

'The heart shot!' said Donaldson to himself and got up stiffly from his rocky hide.

Now, there is a humorous saying to the effect that an elephant never forgets, and though this always evokes mirth, it is nonetheless true. Apart from its phenomenal memory for ordinary things, an elephant never forgets an act of kindness or, conversely, an act of cruelty. There are elephants who after years of absence will recognize an old friend; there are others who will harbour just as long a smouldering hatred against some mahout who has wronged them in the past.

Altogether, the elephant comes of a mysterious race.

Mollie never forgot that it was Kurnail Jarn who had saved her calf.

Kurnail Iarn never recovered fully from the effect of his act of gallantry. He bore with customary fortitude his wounds and the painful stitching and unstitching thereof, and these wounds healed slowly; but Kurnail Jarn's worst hurt was in his back, the muscles of which had been damaged beyond repair by the tiger's strike.

Long after his outward hurts had mended, Kurnail Jarn dragged himself about with difficulty, a shadow of his former robust self.

Not even fresh-baked chappatis made him give tongue now, though he got his fill of them, for Gujar Singh, Donaldson's cook, spoiled him unstintedly.

As for Mollie, she never missed an opportunity of enquiring, in her own peculiar way, for Kurnail Jarn's welfare. If, in her stately progress, she saw Kurnail Jarn taking the sun on the verandah of Donaldson's bungalow, she would put her trunk through the rails and snuff him gently, and sometimes, when the bull-terrier had hobbled out into the compound, Mollie would pick him up with tender care in that same sensitive trunk and place him on her back in front of Parkash Singh, and Kurnail Jarn would ride in state.

As bravely as ever the prick-ears were cocked, the pink tongue lolled eagerly, and you would never have thought from the confident way in which Kurnail Jarn surveyed the jungle from his gently swaying vantage point that his hindquarters were crippled irreparably.

But poor Kurnail Jarn was marked out for tragedy.

He slept by night in a basket at the foot of Donaldson's bed, and while his master snored in exhaustion after another steamy day in the jungle Kurnail Jarn whimpered in his dreams of better days.

One night, soon after Donaldson had turned in, something heavy landed with a thud on the verandah. A long, dark shape bounded through an open door and a brief but violent turmoil ensued in Donaldson's room.

Donaldson, emerging from a tangle of mosquito netting, seized his rifle and his torch. Bhandari Ram, his bearer, rushed in with a lamp.

The first thing they realized was that Kurnail Jarn had vanished and it was obvious that he had not done so under his own propulsion.

'Tiger,' opined Bhandari Ram, sick at the thought of how close the marauder had passed by him.

'Panther,' contradicted Donaldson, and he was right.

The panther has a peculiar and notorious taste for dog-flesh: it is an obsession, a passion, a must, that will often prompt it to reckless action. It was a panther that had seized Kurnail Jarn.

Hurriedly throwing on some clothes, Donaldson, accompanied by Bhandari Ram and the rest of the household which had been roused from their godowns by the hullabaloo, set off on a vain search in the moonlit night.

He soon realized it was hopeless and called off the search.

'Sahib, send for Mahl-ee,' suggested the mahout. 'She smell him out.'

'I wonder,' speculated Donaldson. 'All right; wheel her in.'

It was well known that Mollie, like all her race, had a remarkable sense of smell. One of the servants' favourite games in happier days was to hide a chappattie and hold bets on whether Mollie or Kurnail Iarn would find it first.

Stately and vast in the moonlight, Mollie padded on the scene. Prompted by Bhandari Ram she cast round the bungalow.

Presently, she thumped the ground with her trunk and made steadily off into the jungle, followed by Donaldson and the rest half-running to keep up.

With hardly a check, Mollie followed up the line she had found, only pausing every now and then to give an emphatic thump with her trunk.

A furlong or more from the camp she came to an abrupt halt in front of a tree and would not go on.

'Kurnail Jarn stuck in tree, sahib,' the mahout called back from his perch on Mollie's back.

Donaldson, catching up, caught sight of a tell-tale patch of white in the fork of the tree.

'Poor old Kurnail Jarn,' he murmured. 'He's had it right enough. That's a panther's work beyond all peradventure of a doubt.'

He had to joke; otherwise he would have felt like weeping

for Kurnail Jarn.

As for Mollie, she raised her trunk and tenderly snuffed the body of Kurnail Jarn, just as she had been wont to do when he sunned himself on the verandah.

'The chances are,' Donaldson mused aloud, 'that Spots will return for his booty. I shall sit up and turn myself into a reception committee.'

It was with the utmost difficulty that Mollie could be persuaded to leave Kurnail Jarn. Time after time, she returned to the tree and only by using the goad could her mahout at last force her to march slowly and sadly back to the camp.

Never, thought Donaldson, had he seen an animal so full of grief. The elephant looked quite hunched with sorrow as she went padding through the moonlight attended by the chattering servants.

Meanwhile, he had to find himself a suitable hide. There was no time to build a machan, or platform: he must make do with a handy tree.

Forty yards away from the tree in which Kurnail Jarn's body hung, he found a scaleable perch with an uninterrupted view of that pathetic white patch picked out by the moonlight.

With his back to the bole of the tree and his legs straddling a branch, he settled himself as comfortably as possible for his vigil.

He knew it might be a long one.

The moonlight slid slowly round, but Kurnail Jarn still gleamed faintly.

It was indeed a long and weary wait...

Donaldson's head nodded; he roused up with a painful jerk.

Strive how he might, he could not ward off the leaden feeling that stole into his eyelids.

He dozed...

How long he dozed he did not know. He awoke with a start. In his sleep he thought he had heard something big but stealthy working through the trees. Perhaps, he had been dreaming.

With renewed determination he resumed his watch.

Abruptly, with a thumping heart, in one of those awful jungle silences that came smothering down like something tangible and suffocating, Donaldson knew that the panther had returned.

With every nerve tingling, but with a steady hand, he watched and listened.

Through the moonlit trees to his left, he caught the slightest movement. He dared not turn. He must wait until the panther came into his arc of fire.

The silence was so intense, that it seemed inevitable that either the violent thumping of his heart or the monstrous ticking of his watch would betray him.

His rifle was greasy in his grip and he made a mental note to scold his bearer for leaving too much oil on it, but it was sweat from his hands that he could feel.

Now, from the very corner of his eye, Donaldson knew that the panther was in the open, standing stock-still but for a faint twitching of the tip of its tail. In the bars and filigrees of the moonlight its black rosettes stood out as if embossed.

Still, Donaldson dared not fire. The panther was uneasy and if he tried to bring his gun to bear he would spoil any chance he had in that deceptive light.

As if playing a game of sly fox, the panther glided on a pace and halted, taut and suspicious but lusting for its prey.

Three more paces and Donaldson would fire.

He swallowed...and it seemed a noisy gulp.

Another silent pace and the panther halted, head up, staring, it seemed, straight at Donaldson. It could not have winded him: What little breeze there was came from the direction of Kurnail Jarn's tree.

Donaldson eased the first pressure on the trigger and brought the rifle butt close into his shoulder.

Even as he did so there suddenly burst out of the trees behind him a thundering, trumpeting shape, huge and terrifying in the moonlight.

It was Mollie.

Taken utterly by surprise, for elephant was the last foe it had anticipated—man was what it had suspected—the panther hesitated, and was lost.

It flattened in the jungle grass, turned, bellied away too late.

One huge and terrible foot bowled it over; a second huge and terrible foot broke its back.

And, snarling hideously in brief agony, the panther was pounded and crushed and utterly obliterated beneath the stamping feet of Mollie.

In his tree, Donaldson watched and wondered, breathless with awe at this savage spectacle. Whether Mollie had come back to mourn her lost friend, or whether she had deliberately set out to ambush the panther, he could not tell.

But all that did not matter: The effect was the same.

Kurnail Jarn had been avenged.